I0633284

The Iron Dog

Carme, McAlistair Mysteries, Book Three

Liz Graham

OneEar Press

For information, please visit the author website LizGraham.ca or email at
Liz@LizGraham.ca

ISBN: 978-1-990667-20-6

Chapter 1

Sometimes life offers you a second chance, no matter how badly you mess up the first time round. Of course, sometimes life requires that you create that second chance yourself, if you really want it.

And so, Carmel McAlistair found herself again in the company of Inspector John Darrow of the Royal Newfoundland Constabulary. Their first date had been rudely interrupted which was totally her fault, yet after months of silence, she'd found him again.

All she'd had to do was engineer a chance meeting outside her new place of work, The Rooms. This huge building housed the province's art galleries and archives where she now worked, and it just happened to be next door to the constabulary headquarters. In fact, when Carmel craned her neck and peered out the west window she could look straight into Darrow's office, if it weren't for the smoked glass windows of the RNC building.

By carefully timing her trips to the coffee shop behind the headquarters, she soon contrived an accidental meeting and it was all plain sailing from there. Well, it would be once she showed him she wouldn't run out on him again.

Carmel dressed with special care that evening, re-wetting her brown curls so they were glossy and just so, and even wearing a bit of make up to enhance her blue eyes and freckled complexion. Although they hadn't planned anything fancy——just a movie, an art documentary at that. Sort of nerdy, yes, but John Darrow was her date.

After the movie let out, the two of them wandered from the theatre to the main part of the mall, still crowded as the evening was still early. A band of young musicians played Celtic-influenced music which echoed through the atrium with a yearning wistful tone, harking back to better times, more romantic times. Their backdrop was draped with a huge old Irish tri-color flag known to many as the Pink, White and Green.

"There's that flag again," Darrow noted as they paused at the railing. "It seems to be everywhere all of a sudden. Do you think the musicians are the cultural arm of the Newfoundland Liberation Army?"

Carmel laughed. "The NLA. I've seen their posters around town, on all the lamp-posts and abandoned store-fronts downtown," she said. "Are they really that organized? I thought the whole movement was just one of those flash in the pan, university student things."

He nodded. "They haven't come across my desk yet," he said. "I believe they're dreamers rather than doers."

"I can't imagine anyone really wants us to break apart," Carmel said. "We're far too tiny an island to survive on our own."

"Care for a coffee?" Darrow asked, his hand warming the small of her back. They took the escalator down to the coffee shop, one side opened to the flow of passers-by as if it was a cafe in Paris.

On the way, he described an odd case he'd been called to that day. "A body was found under Water Street today," he said. "In a bricked up cellar on the old Clerkwell property."

The Clerkwells were an old moneyed family in St. John's who'd grown their business from the fishing trade over the centuries. Their original premises had been on the corner of Water and Prescott Streets, backing onto the harbor, and when the original wooden structure had burned down in the 1840's, it had been rebuilt with a fine stone building. Unfortunately, the salt air had eaten into the mortar and the location had gone out of fashion in the 1970's, and the building had been left unloved for many years until it became a public hazard and was razed to the ground. Now the empty lot had been sold for millions of dollars and a hotel was to be constructed on the spot.

"What do you mean, under Water Street?"

"Back in the day, they used every available bit of space," he said, his Scottish accent coming through as he spoke. "The water was closer then, a lot of the harbor has been reclaimed over the years. They had nowhere to expand, so I guess they figured the land under the street was fair game. It wasn't being used, after all, and no-one would be the wiser if they dug it out. Sometimes whole tunnels were constructed beneath the streets, connecting the old cellars between houses and businesses.

"This particular cellar had been covered up with the stone foundations when the mid-nineteenth century building was constructed," Darrow continued. "It was only unearthed today."

"So, the body––was it murder?" Carmel asked, a spark of curiosity in her eye. She and Darrow had met over murder, so to speak, the previous summer. He understood her interest.

He handed her the paper coffee cup, accidently brushing her hand with his own. She felt a spark, like a blue electric flush warm her hand and quickly glanced up at his face. He'd maybe felt it too, for he wore an almost smile on his face and his brown eyes were curiously vulnerable.

"Definitely murder," Darrow replied as they sat at a table. "A skeleton by now, of course, but the knife was still in the ribcage, hidden by his heavy woolen coat."

They took seats outside, side by side, facing the passing world of the mall while they removed their winter jackets. He wore a light knit sweater over his shirt and tie, the dark red complimenting his dark complexion and brown eyes. There wasn't a lot of elbow room, but Carmel didn't mind being pressed close to him. In fact, she snuggled a bit, causing him to smile and put his arm around the back of her chair.

"The body was huddled over a wooden chest," he noted.

"I wonder what that was about. You think he was defending the chest?"

"It would seem to be, but we'll never know the story now," he said. "Our Mr. Doe dates from two hundred years ago. Samples from his clothing will be sent away for testing to be sure, but the new stone foundations were laid in 1840, and his clothing looks to predate that."

"So what was in the chest that he was guarding? Was it a treasure chest?"

Darrow laughed. "One man's trash may be another man's treasure," he said. "But there was nothing inside except for old clothes and part of a map."

"Surely it's a treasure map, at least?" Carmel's face showed her disappointment.

"No 'X' to mark the spot, sorry to say," he replied. "Just a scrap of paper, really. However, from what I saw, it did look like the cove you live in."

St. Jude Without was Carmel's adopted home where she had bought a house when she'd returned to the province last summer. Although located only a twenty minute drive outside the city of St. John's, it was the island's best kept secret, as if its inhabitants purposefully flew under the radar of mainstream society. Originally settled by the pirate Jeremy Ryan, his descendants kept up the family tradition of leading shady lives.

"You think it's Captain Jem's body?" Her eyes lit up. Her home was the old pirate's original house, the first built in the cove, and he was rumored to still haunt the space. Legend had it that he had been lynched on the old pine tree right outside Carmel's front door, then his body tarred and left to rot on Gibbet Hill overlooking the city as a warning to pirates everywhere. Carmel hadn't actually met his ghost yet and preferred to ignore any odd happenings in her home for she didn't believe in the supernatural. If it was Jem's body that had been found in the old cellar under Water Street, then he hadn't died outside his house and she had no reason to fear his ghost.

"No way to tell," Darrow said,."unless we do a DNA analysis of the skeleton and his descendants––your Ryan friends in the cove. But I doubt the budget will stretch to that."

She nodded in understanding.

"However, you should have a chance to look at it yourself," he continued. "The chest will be arriving at the museum tomorrow, and I guess the map will go to the archives. Also, when the lab is finished with the knife, it will be a great, if rather grisly, addition to the museum. It's a cutlass, a fine example of its kind."

"What? Like a big curved pirate sword?"

He laughed. She could feel it deep through his sweater. "Not the scimitar that Hollywood portrays. The cutlass is actually a small sword, sharp and ideal for slashing ropes or fighting at close quarters," he said. "Must have been quite the thrust to lodge it deep inside a man's ribcage."

"Funny coincidences, then. A pirate's cutlass and a map of St. Jude Without, which was founded by a pirate."

The conversation was interrupted as a body parted from the milling throng and lazily took the seat across from Carmel.

"David!" David Clerkwell was Carmel's immediate boss at the archives. A scion of the original Clerkwell family, he was reputed to be a brilliant young man and next in line for the position of head archivist when the present incumbent retired, if she ever did.

The city of St. John's was like a small town, the populace tightly woven together through families and neighborhoods. Carmel's good friend Rhonda was David's cousin, and had confided that he was considered very odd by the family. He'd seemed okay to Carmel so far though, perhaps more concerned with his work than with the people around him, at least when he was engrossed in a project. Single-minded and intense, that was the best way to describe him, so perhaps Rhonda might be right in her off-the-cuff diagnosis of Asperger's.

David was a physically perfect man with flawless skin and his sleek black hair cut in a bob just at the nape of his neck––many women spent hours trying to achieve that natural shine. David draped his tall slim frame with a long coat and a brightly colored wool scarf, achieving an easy elegance and presence that few academics could dream of, looking more like he'd stepped from the pages of Vogue than from an archive's dusty aisles.

"Mind if I join you for a moment?" He already had, and he shifted his chair to better view the wide aisle where people still flowed. David did have a peculiarity in that he rarely made eye contact with those he was speaking to. He had the most luminous gray eyes, fringed with almost criminally lush long black lashes, the sort of eyes that drew your attention and made you want to pause in their depths. Shyness might account for his unwillingness to make eye contact with people.

Carmel made quick introductions. "David, this is John Darrow." David's eyes characteristically nodded in a smiling swoop about their heads without landing as he nodded and shook Darrow's hand.

"I was just saying that my house was built by a pirate."

"Folk legends, my dear," David said in a kind voice as he watched the flow of people around them.

"No, this is true," Carmel laughed. "At least according to the residents of St. Jude Without. And they're all direct descendants of him, so they should know."

David's gaze swerved from the crowd and honed in on her, taking her by surprise. "St. Jude Without?"

"It's a little cove north of Portugal Cove," she explained. "Most people have never heard of it."

"Au contraire, my friend," he said, drawing closer to her across the table. "Are you talking about Captain Ryan? You live in Jeremy Ryan's house?"

For the first time she noticed that the gray of his eyes was darkly outlined in black around the edges of the corneas. A person could get lost in those eyes, drawn in and chewed up and spit out without a second's thought. No wonder he avoided eye contact. People were messy, and it wasn't his fault.

"Yeah, the old stone and clapboard cottage in the middle of the cove."

He blinked and his gaze quickly went back across the mall. "Well, well. Imagine that. I must come visit someday," he said. David seared her with another glancing look and a smile. "I do like pirates, you know."

He took his leave shortly after without getting a coffee, restless as ever, and they watched as he moved back into the swimming crowd.

"He's an odd duck," said Carmel. "But I quite like him."

"David is from the Clerkwell family, isn't he?" Darrow mused.

"Yes," said Carmel. "He's related to my friend Rhonda, the doctor. There's a lot of money in that family."

"If you go back far enough, everyone in this town is related, especially those with money," he said with just a hint of cynicism coming through in his Scots accent.

Chapter 2

C armel was to learn, in good time, that one of the reasons Darrow had left his native Scotland was to escape the claustrophobic class system which still permeated the upper echelons of every institution, even after all these years. He could easily have used his own family connections to sweep up to the top of his profession there, but what he saw on the way to the top had sickened him. Canada with its wide spaces and promise of equality had beckoned, so it was ironic that he'd landed right in the most colonial of provinces, the last holdout of the British Empire which had been dragged kicking and screaming into North America in the middle of the last century. The class system was alive and well here in St. John's.

As they walked hand-in-hand to her car in the lightly falling snow, the two were silent. Carmel for her part was thinking she couldn't be happier, yet she was loath for the evening to end, and her steps slowed as they reached her old sedan. In the blue of the parking lot lights, you could hardly notice the rust creeping up the side of the driver's side door.

"Well, here I am," she said, reluctance in her voice, but her face brightened when he took her in his arms and held her.

"I hope you don't think I'm rushing things," he said in a soft voice. He was a couple of inches taller than her, maybe three, the perfect height for her to rest her face on his shoulder. But not for long. She felt his head move towards her and lifted her own up for this kiss, this long awaited meeting of lips, and it was everything she'd been waiting for.

Hah. In Carmel's rather limited experience, rushing things was meeting in a late night bar, getting sozzled and basing a long-term relationship on alcohol, then trying to pick up the pieces when it all inevitably collapsed two years later. Darrow was painstakingly slow. This was delicious anticipation.

A long moment after, he lifted his head again and met her eyes, his hand reaching up to brush the snow from her brown curls with his bare hand.

"I enjoyed this evening," he said. "I'd like to do it again."

She couldn't contain the smile on her face.

"But it's important to me for you to know what you may be getting tangled up with," he said. "You know I have children?"

Carmel was aware, having seen the photo in his office, a boy and a girl, but no wife in that picture.

"And the mother of your kids?" He had never brought up his marriage, she didn't know if there was an ex, if he was a widower, or if he was even still married.

He laughed and hugged her. "Don't worry. Fiona fled back to Scotland years ago. She didn't like the Canadian winters."

Oh good, so the ex-wife wasn't even in the country. That made things much easier. "I'd like to see you again," she said.

They said their good-byes for the night and he let her go, then she got in the car and tried to start it. And tried, and tried again, but nothing happened. She heard a tap on her window.

"I'm not an expert," Darrow said when she rolled down the window, "but it sounds like the ignition's not catching."

The thirteen-year-old Corolla was rusty but usually reliable. However, like a geriatric mule it was arthritic and testy, and sometimes balked for reasons of its own.

"Oh!" Carmel cried, hitting the steering wheel with both hands. "This stupid car. I'll have to call Bridget or Phonse to come pick me up."

"Nonsense," he said, opening her door. "I'll take you back."

She got out of the sedan, her eyes never leaving his. Ooh, this was more like it. She patted the car door and silently thanked it.

As he drove, he opened up about his past, how Fiona had insisted on having two children to make her life complete, and then had changed her mind, claiming she couldn't be tied down.

"Where is she now?"

"I honestly don't know," he said. "Last we heard she was at Kloster's for the skiing. But I have the kids, Danielle and Angus, so she can go wherever she likes for all I care."

It was a comfortable ride in his SUV despite the pot-holed gravel road of St. Jude Without. The entire cove was silent and almost black except for the lights on at the church, and there seemed to be no eyes watching as she entered her house with Darrow in tow. She waited until he had gone through the porch, then quickly pulled the blind down on the glass window of the door––an accepted signal to the other residents in the cove not to barge in; she'd never had a chance to test its effectiveness before.

Carmel busied herself lighting the fire, dimming the lights (not too much, of course, but a girl had to create atmosphere) and getting drinks, while he made a phone call to check on his family. She brought the two whiskies in to the living room just as he ended the call.

"I just touched base with Mrs. O'Keefe," he said, not quite meeting her eyes as he loosened his tie. "She's the surrogate mother who runs my household. I'm fortunate––she has the apartment in the back of our house, which has come in handy for child care over the years with my schedule."

"Always someone to keep an eye on the kids, despite you being a single parent?"

"She's a jewel."

Hmmm. Perhaps he was hinting that this freed him up from making the long drive back to town. He'd loosened his tie, and that was a very good sign. Carmel sat next to him on the old red sofa, acting more confident than she felt. "It's getting nasty out there," she noted. The wind whistled up the open flue in agreement.

"And it's rather cozy in here," he agreed, placing his arm around her. She remembered his smell, one of spices and lemons and him, and lay her head against him, the better to breathe him in.

This wasn't considered a first date, was it? She liked John Darrow, a lot. Besides, they'd known each other since last summer. Rushing it? Would he think she was too forward if she invited him to stay the night? This sort of thing had been a lot easier years ago in her twenties. She no longer knew what the dating game rules were.

Carmel decided she would have to just come out and ask him. She lifted his head just as he moved his, and their lips met again for the second time that evening. Ah, now this was bliss.

Many long moments later, he paused to remove the thin sweater and loosen his tie further.

"Why don't you just take that off," she murmured, leaning her head back to watch him with a smile on her face, sure of her ground now.

"The tie?" he said. "Ach, that never comes off until I go to bed." He smiled, his brown eyes glinting warm in the firelight.

"If that's what it takes, then..."

But she didn't get to finish her lazy teasing, for the room was pierced with a pop song in midstream, a Bollywood girl band she'd never heard before, the words not in English but unmistakable in their angst.

"What on earth is that?"

Darrow groaned and hauled himself forward, reaching into his coat pocket. "That is the end of this night, I'm afraid," he said over the noise. "I knew it was too good to last."

"What is the problem?" His voice was stern and thoroughly pissed off. She wouldn't want to be the person at the other end of that line. "You're not alone; Mrs. O'Keefe is next door."

Yet his tone didn't deter the caller. Carmel could hear the plaintive voice coming through, rising in pitch.

He leaned his elbows on his knees, pinching the top of his nose with his free hand. "She's a trained nurse; she can do more for you than I can." He listened as the other cut in. "Well, stop doing it if it makes you throw up!" He hung on with a sigh.

"I'm afraid she's not ready for this," he said to Carmel, apology and frustration wrestling in his voice.

Carmel hugged her feet up on to the sofa. "Kids, huh?"

"She's fifteen years old; this is ridiculous," he said, yet he stood and hauled the sweater back over his head. "Don't get me wrong," he continued. "I love the child. She was unlucky enough to inherit my looks, but she's the spit of her mother all the same. She can't help being the way she is."

Carmel stood up alongside him and placed her arms around him. "It's okay." She said it to his sweater to hide her disappointment. "Perhaps we need to take it slower. We have lots of time."

She could feel his groan rumble through his chest. He held her by the arms so as to look her in the eyes. "They do go to their mother's in the summer," he said.

Summer is a long way away, Carmel thought.

Chapter 3

S o Darrow had left and she was alone. It was way too early to go to bed and, besides, she wouldn't be able to sleep, not now. A drink and some mindless chatter would help, and she knew where to find that close at hand.

The rosette window was glowing in the old church next door, so the usual congregation would be gathered for their nightly beers and gossip. Built the year after Captain Jeremy Ryan had died, the old building had been deconsecrated and sold to Sid's father once the population had declined and people had stopped their regular church-going habits. He'd used it for storage, but when Sid inherited it, he quit his good job at the Coast Guard and lived the dream of owning his own pub. Few renovations had been required, and the church had never been as popular as it was now.

As she reached the door, her attention was caught by a flag flapping overhead in the strong breeze, strung up on the wooden bell tower of the old church. Carmel craned her neck in the moonlight and saw the pink, green and white looming over her. A political statement was a rare thing in St. Jude Without, and unsettling in a way. Her neighbors never cared who or what party was in government, as long as they were left alone to do their nefarious businesses.

The usual crowd sat in their usual places with Clyde the farmer in the corner with his enormous black dog by his side, the pool-players off to Carmel's right, the bikers off to her left with their black leather coats all endowed with the feathered hat which was their insignia. Bridget and her cousin Phonse were in deep conversation on the stools by the bar. Sid presided as usual behind the altar-turned-bar, the Christmas lights around the apse framing his tall thin body and he was joined by a third person, a man as yet unknown to Carmel.

A beer appeared before her as she approached, handed to her with a silent nod by Sid. The light coming up through the thin granite sheet which served as the counter lit the planes of his face, highlighting his handle bar moustache and shadowing his eyes. He never said much, but knew everything that was happening in the cove.

Carmel looked over towards her friends. The two cousins were huddled over Phonse's phone, he laughing uproariously, while she scowled at the screen.

"That's really stupid," the thirty-something red-head said, turning her trim body away from him. She flicked her long hennaed hair in disgust.

"What're ya talking about? That's the funniest thing I ever saw!" He looked up and seeing Carmel, beckoned her over. "Come look at this!"

A video played on the tiny screen of Phonse's new phone. A long white air balloon, a company mascot perhaps, danced in the snow with its tiny arms outstretched. The poor thing had been bent by the wind and caught its head on a telephone wire, causing it to shake its booty over and over and over in an endless dance. Carmel watched it in silence as he cracked up again.

"Yeah, it's funny," Carmel said. "Sort of."

"It might be funny for three seconds," Bridget cut in. "Moptop here has been watching it for five minutes and he still finds it hilarious." She turned to him. "You have the brains of a guppy."

Phonse ignored her jibes and moved closer to Carmel. Last summer her body would have thrilled at the contact with this gorgeous fisherman with his bright blue eyes and blond curls just slightly graying, but she had gotten to know him better since then. At forty-five years of age, he was not relationship material, for he was happy to remain perpetually young with his drinking buddies and hold no responsibility whatsoever.

"Where were you tonight?" Bridget asked her. "You missed the darts tournament." Her boyfriend Ian was touring with his garage punk/ traditional band, so she was at a loose end.

"Oh, I had a date," Carmel replied, leaving it at that. She purposely didn't mention that she'd spent the evening with Inspector Darrow of the Royal Newfoundland Constabulary, for the crowd in the cove could be strange about cops.

"A date?" Phonse finally looked up from his phone. "If you're looking for company, my offer still stands." He put his arm around her and pulled her close.

"Get off," she said, shrugging away from him. Attractive as he might be physically, she had no desire to become the second Mrs. Ryan. The first was his mother Vee who he still lived with, and who hated Carmel with a passion. Carmel didn't much like Vee either.

"How's the job?" Bridget now wanted to know. Phonse returned to his phone to look for more funny videos.

"Great," said Carmel. "It's part-time, so I still have time to write, but at least it'll help with the mortgage." Until very recently, Carmel had been a freelance travel writer, but she'd gotten tired of the endless deadlines and flights and changes in time zone. She wanted a quiet life for a change, so when the job at the Archives had appeared, she'd grabbed it.

"And tomorrow should be pretty exciting," she continued. "An old wooden chest was found in a cellar under Water Street and they'll be bringing it up to the museum."

Bridget sipped her beer and didn't look too impressed.

"There was a map inside the chest," Carmel told her. "And I'm told it might be of St. Jude Without. How weird is that?"

Bridget straightened up and whirled around on her stool to look directly at Carmel. "Where was this chest found?"

"On the old Clerkwell property," Carmel told her. "Where there's been an empty lot for years."

"What?" Bridget was terse. "On the corner of Water Street and Prescott?"

"That's the one," Carmel replied. "You know they're building there, right? A new hotel is going up finally. Well, hidden behind the foundations of the 1840's stone building, they found an old chest in the cellar. It's probably from way back in the early 1800's."

"Phonse! Listen to this." She gave her cousin a sharp elbow to his ribs.

Surprised at Bridget's reaction, Carmel repeated her story again for Phonse's benefit.

The two Ryan cousins looked extremely perturbed.

"Did you say there was a map inside it?" Phonse asked. He darted a glance at Bridget.

"The Clerkwell premises," Bridget repeated slowly. "The one on the waterfront."

"Tell me it didn't have a skeleton with it," Phonse said, a note of hope in his voice.

"Yeah," Carmel said, looking at him in astonishment. "It did. How'd you know?"

Bridget bit her lip while Phonse remained silent for once.

"It's an old family legend," Bridget said at last. "Just a bit of foolishness, I'm sure." The two stared at each other again, unable to hide the distress in their eyes.

"Come on, you can't leave me dangling like this," Carmel said. "Tell me what's on the go. Why do you guys care about a two hundred year old map?"

"Well, the chest and the skeleton, they were found on the Clerkwell premises, right?"

Carmel nodded at Phonse's words. "And?"

"Jem Ryan used to work for the Clerkwells."

"I thought he was a pirate," Carmel said.

"Yeah, well, that was his second career," Phonse agreed. "Bridget––you know this story better. You tell it."

"You sure about this Phonse?" his cousin asked.

"She's living in Cap'n Jem's house, for God's sake," he said. "Surely she has a right to know the whole story. Even if she hasn't met him yet."

"Hello? She is still here, guys. What do I need to know about my house?" Carmel asked. "And who have I not yet met?"

Bridget let out a sigh. "All right then. The story goes that Jeremy Ryan came over to the island as a boy on a fishing vessel. From Ireland. He'd been taken from the streets of Dublin and forced into labor by the Clerkwell gang, as he was an orphan and living rough."

"That's horrible," Carmel said.

"Yeah, well, that's the way it was back then," Bridget answered. "Anyway, he got into the life at sea and found it suited him."

Young Jeremy Ryan had risen through the ranks of the Clerkwell fleet until he found himself captain of their main ship, the Portugal Rose. The Clerkwells were a hard crowd, well known to be a bunch of thieves and scallywags as was common in some of the families who rose to prominence and wealth during the late 1700's off the shores of the island. Their business practices were no better and no worse than most others.

Anyway, as Bridget told the story, the family finally angered Jeremy for the last time by devaluing his whole year's catch of fish and paying far less than the amount expected. This affected not just the captain but his entire crew who depended on their shares of the annual haul.

Ryan didn't just fly off the handle and go on a murdering rampage, however; he waited for the perfect opportunity to get his revenge. When the bride-to-be of the oldest Clerkwell son was being transported overseas from England with her dowry and finery on the Portugal Rose, he commandeered the ship.

Stole it, in other words, turning pirate as he did so.

He also stole the fair lady's heart. Well, eventually he did, as it was a long voyage with not a lot else for a lady to do.

The two travelled the seas, hell-bent on the ruination of the Clerkwell line and all the other fishing admirals from the coasts of Newfoundland right down to the Bahamas. They made their base in Bermuda until he figured it was time to settle down and quit pirating. He found the hidden cove of St. Jude Without and built the house for his––by then––large family of off-spring. The very same house Carmel bought last fall.

"Yet, the story goes, for all the thieving he did, he never touched her dowry. He wanted her to have it in case anything happened to him, but poor old Eliza never got a chance."

"What happened to it?"

Bridget and Phonse shared another of their enigmatic cousinly looks.

"There's two endings to that story," the redhead told her. "You know that Jeremy was lynched right on the old pine tree by your house, right?"

"Yeah." Carmel gave a shiver of distaste. She'd always hated knowing that about the stump that still stood by her door.

"It was a Clerkwell, the second son who became a priest, who led the lynch mob that killed Jem," Phonse noted.

"We've always assumed the chest containing her dowry and jewels was taken then and there," said Bridget. "However..."

The other ending to the story was that the Clerkwell priest who stole the chest got nothing but Jem's old cast-off clothing for his trouble and half a map that might have told where to find the treasure, if one knew how to read it and if one had the other half of the map. Jem's loyal right-hand man did, and set off to retrieve the map after the pirate's body was left to rot on Gibbet Hill. Nothing else was ever heard of him again, so all assumed he'd been killed. The priest himself died a couple of years later in an unrelated drunken brawl on George Street, after he had constructed the church next door to Jem's house.

Carmel took a swallow of beer as the realization sank in. "And now they've found a chest containing old clothes and a map buried in a bricked up cellar on the old Clerkwell premises..."

Her two companions nodded, excitement like a glow around them.

"I guess Jem's friend must have confronted the priest, who killed him too," said Bridget.

"With his own sword..." Carmel added, remembering Darrow's words.

"So he must have hidden the body and the chest in the disused cellar until he figured out what to do about it," Phonse chipped in.

"But got himself killed in a fight, before he got round to doing something about the body," Carmel added, caught up in the excitement now.

"So he never got a chance to return." Bridget nodded. "And after the fire, the Clerkwells rebuilt the building with new stone foundations, blocking up that old cellar until now. I guess the priest never told his family what he'd done."

"Which means..."

"It's a treasure map!" Phonse burst out, unable to contain himself any longer. "It's Captain Jem's treasure map!"

Before Carmel could disabuse him of that notion, the man who'd been speaking with Sid spoke up. He had drifted over to the small group while they'd been talking and listened in.

"That, my friend," he pronounced in a deep, gravelly voice, "that is very interesting. Phonse, we got to get on that." He was a tall guy with a shaggy beard and a man bun, dressed in a heavy lumberjack shirt and boots, but just a little too dishevelled to carry off the hipster look.

"Yeah, Nate, what do you think? That would take care of a few issues, huh? Right?" Phonse looked excited as a puppy.

"Nate, you haven't met Carmel yet," Bridget said. "This is Sid's cousin, back from the mainland."

"Dr. Ignatius O'Reilly, at your service," he said as he gave a mock bow.

A doctor? She looked at the greasy head bowed in front of her. If he was a medical doctor, it looked like he'd skipped the class on hygiene. But she didn't say what was on her mind.

"You're not a Ryan?" Carmel was one of the few inhabitants of the cove not to share the Ryan last name. Everyone was related here.

"Oh, yes, I am," he replied, "but on my mother's side."

"He's a doctor, eh?" Phonse pointed out to her in case she'd missed the fact. "We're proud of him. First of the Ryans to go through university." The two guys clinked their beer mugs.

"Yeah, I've joined the ranks of the over-educated unemployed," Nate said in his rough voice. "A PhD in Colonial history––you'd think I could get a job here. But the crowd of mainlanders up at the university only want to hire CFAs; native Newfoundlanders aren't good enough for them. We need to get local people in places of power at the cultural institutions or we're just continuing the cycle, generation after generation." This had the sound of a well-rehearsed complaint.

The term CFAs, or 'Come-From-Aways' denoted anyone who was not born in the province, or who didn't at least have family connections to the place. Also known as 'Mainlanders,' most of these folk moved to the province because they loved the beauty and wilderness of the island and appreciated the relaxed life style missing from their own crowded homelands in North America or elsewhere in the world.

It sounded as if Nate had a particular bee in his bonnet and Carmel knew he must be responsible for the independence flag flying over the church.

"So, how do you propose to go about changing things?" she challenged him. These dreamers didn't usually have a solid plan in place.

"Well, Carmel," he said as he leaned a bit closer and she got a whiff of beer and cigarette smoke. "Life has a way of working out for those who help themselves."

The gleam of intelligence in his eyes caught her by surprise, Yet really, she thought, it shouldn't. He had managed to get a doctoral degree from somewhere, so there was more to the man than just husky good looks and dreams and a smell of uncleanliness.

Nate stepped back and opened his undone shirt to show his black t-shirt. It was embossed with another replica of the flag along with the letters NLA transposed over in dripping red paint. The official t-shirt of the Newfoundland Liberation Army. "What do we say?" he roared too close to her ear. She winced.

"N-L-A!" Phonse yelled, echoing in response like Pavlov's dog. He turned to the rest of the bar and called over the AC/DC playing on the stereo and rose his mug into the air again. "Free Newfoundland!"

A few of the regulars lifted their mugs in half-hearted solidarity then turned back to their conversations.

"Well, this is one Newfoundlander who has found a job," Carmel told Nate. She found the whole Independence movement a little tiresome with their single-minded agenda and surprising lack of practical plans. God forbid they ever won an election and formed the government. "I'm working at the Archives."

"The Archives," Nate said, ruminating in his rumbly voice. "I know them well. I spent many a long hour there as a student." He laughed, but it was unpleasant. "I worked there. That old bag Marcia still in charge? What a crank. You know she fired me?"

"Oh?" Not really surprising. Carmel knew that Marcia Flynn, the head archivist, wasn't very popular among her staff and definitely wasn't the warm and fuzzy type of woman. The little she'd seen of the archivist showed her to be a grouchy, rude snob who looked down on anyone who didn't have her level of education. She also insisted her staff be pleasant, polite and neatly dressed––none of which applied to Nate. "Maybe now you have a PhD, she might like you more."

"Nah, she objected to me smoking dope out on the fire escape," Nate chortled. Phonse laughed with him, on cue. "Man, I know that place like the back of my hand. All the places to hide away in so she couldn't see I wasn't working. Oh man, those were the days."

"So what are your plans now?" Carmel asked, although she was itching to end this conversation and get away from him.

"Just you wait and see, baby," he replied in his rough gravelly voice. He actually winked as he said it. "Shag that, I'm not sucking up to the likes of that mainlander just for a paycheque. I'm going to make my own job."

Carmel winced again. He might be educated, but those years at university hadn't smoothed out his rough edges.

"Newfoundland for the Newfoundlanders," he said. He and Phonse raised their beers yet again.

She rolled her eyes behind their backs and slipped off her stool, preparing to go back home. Before she could leave, Phonse caught her arm in a firm grip.

"You need to get me that map," he whispered. "Nate needs it."

"Nate can wait till it's processed and available for the public, just like everybody else," she said, trying to shrug him off.

"You don't understand," he continued in a low voice. "This is really important. It's our heritage. He has big plans, and he needs money behind him."

"I'm not going to steal something from my place of work," she whispered back at him, furious.

"Geez, Carmel, I'm not asking you to steal anything," Phonse said, his eyes widening in innocence. "Just... just get a copy of it for me. I want to surprise him."

This took Carmel aback. Phonse was one of the most self-centred and self-indulgent people she knew, and this might be the first time she'd heard him express a desire to help someone else. "Okay," she nodded, after considering a moment. "I'll try to get a copy for you. It sounds like it's Captain Jem's map, after all."

He released her arm and grinned.

"Hey," she said to him. "I need a ride into town bright and early tomorrow."

"You promise to get me that map, and it's a deal."

She forgot to tell him that Darrow had said it wasn't a treasure map. Never mind, he'd find out soon enough.

Carmel walked the few steps back to her home quickly, huddled against the rising north wind which cut like a knife through the seams of her coat. As she reached her front steps, her attention was caught by the rustling of the lilac tree, its leafless branches clacking together in the rising gale. The ancient pine stump next to it glowed whitely in the dark.

She shivered as she opened the front door and closed it firmly behind her, determined not to think about the stories of Captain Jem's ghost which Phonse had poured in her ear the previous summer. She hadn't yet met the pirate and had no intention of doing so if she could help it. As if ghosts existed.

Speaking of which, she noticed that yet again Captain Jem's red book Pirates of Newfoundlande was sticking out of the living room book shelf where she tried to keep it. The book had a habit of popping off its shelf and appearing elsewhere in the house. It was Phonse and his stupid tricks, she knew, his small attempt to scare her into believing his ghost stories. Perhaps she should foil him and start locking her doors. Carmel slammed the book back into place.

"And stay there," she muttered.

Chapter 4

P honse blew his horn outside her house to pick her up before eight o'clock and then went on to collect Nate from the church next door.

Large-boned and hairy, Nate squished into the front seat of the old truck next to Carmel, taking up way more room than he was entitled to. She was forced into the middle with the uncomfortable plastic fold-down arm rest against her back and tried not to let her hips press against either man. Nate smelled as if he'd spent the night on the bar floor.

In fact, there was also the distinct smell of stale dope throughout the truck. Not being by a window, she just had to suffer through it.

"What are you doing in town today, Nate?" she asked.

"Oh, I got plans," he said. "Got to meet a guy at Tim Horton's. You know, bring down the government, start the revolution. Usual things."

Both men laughed as if his words were funnier than the mascot shaking its booty on Phonse's phone, and they high fived within Carmel's personal space, squashing her even more. She fumed silently at the two buffoons.

But then Phonse started in on his questioning of Carmel, not letting up for the whole twenty minute drive into the city. Someone must have spotted the unknown SUV outside her house the previous evening and Phonse's blue eyes were tinged with green. Vee must have filled him in when he got home last night.

"Darrow, the cop?" Phonse couldn't believe what he was hearing. "And he lit out in the middle of the night without even offering you a ride back to your car? That's not the behaviour of a man who cares, Carmel."

"It wasn't close to the middle of the night," she retorted. "Remember, I dropped round to the bar after. And we didn't... and it's none of your business anyway." She sat back in the seat and tried to fold her arms, but Nate was not giving her much room to move.

"It is too my business," Phonse said. "I thought we had a thing going on here. You're cheating on me. And with a cop!" This was the worst betrayal he could imagine.

She flat out refused to answer that one. There was not, nor had there ever been, a 'thing' between them. A long-dead crush did not count as a relationship.

He pulled off Thorburn Road and into the Mall parking lot, tearing around the turns as if on his way to a fire, the truck's back wheels slipping a little on the leftover ice. "There." Phonse stopped short in front of Carmel's lonely blue sedan.

"Aren't you guys going to help?"

"Doubt if there's much wrong with your car. You probably just pretended there was to drag him off," he said, then raised his voice in a terrible girly impersonation. "Oh, Inspector Darrow, my darn old car won't work. I need you to save me!"

Stung speechless, Carmel stuttered to find the words to tell him what an obnoxious jerk he was.

"Well, are you going to try it? The car won't start itself."

Nate only moved his legs a bit so she was forced to gracelessly climb over him in order to exit the truck. She slammed the door of the filthy vehicle and stomped over to her car. With the key in the ignition, it started on the first try. "It really wasn't working," she shouted as she unwound the window. But the guys were already driving off in a spurt of snow thrown up behind their truck.

***

That morning, it was Darrow's turn for the office coffee run at the Tim Horton's next door to the RNC headquarters. It was a delicate operation which had to be timed just right for maximum efficiency. Any time after 8:20 and the 9-5 workers arrived all at once for their caffeine fixes and the line stretched throughout the coffee shop, snaking round itself among the tables and chairs in an impatient swarm. Before 8 a.m. and the change of shift, the line was short but the wait seemed endless as the tired night staff tried to get everything ready for the day ahead.

He was late getting down to the coffee shop today. As he stood in line, he surveyed the crowd around him with a practiced eye. There in the far corner were the boarding house men––kicked out of their respective boarding houses at 7:30 a.m. and looking to fill the day until they were allowed back in for the evening meal. Ahead of him in the lineup, were two young secretaries tottering in high heels and tight skirts, their make-up perfect and hair ironed flat. A solid lawyer dressed in his court clothes waited ahead of them, while at the table by Darrow's side sat a man writing in his notebook, oblivious to the world around him, an author of local fame.

In his sweep around the store, his eye was caught by a man who was studiously ignoring him, hand covering his face as if to hide it from Darrow's glare. He knew that dark face. Ruscan Milanovic. The Inspector's eyes narrowed as they settled on this foreign nationalist. Carmel's ex-lover. The one who had disappeared mid-flight, then shown up in her life a year later, right in the middle of their New Year's Eve date. She had taken off in a tearing hurry and he hadn't seen her again till their chance meeting here in the coffee shop last week.

Darrow had been keeping tabs on Ruscan, naturally. He was familiar with the Interpol reports from Europe, the dealings with the Russian mafia-type organizations, the status of his refugee claim, where the man was staying and anyone he had contact with. This was unofficial surveillance, of course, which he filed under the 'Public Safety' budget.

He didn't recognize Milanovic's companion, though. Darrow craned his neck a little to inspect the man, not even bothering to be discreet for it did no harm to let the Ukranian know he was being watched. The other man was broad of shoulder, with a beard and long greasy hair straggling over his red and black checked jacket. The sound of his deep voice rumbled through the coffee shop though his words were muffled. A local, by the sounds of it, and Darrow had a gut instinct the two were up to no good.

Ruscan hunched over the table, urging the other to take what he was palming, but his companion was shaking his head and pushing back. This would bear watching, and Darrow filed this away in his mind.

Chapter 5

O n her way to the archive room, Carmel paused for a moment to catch her breath. There were a lot of stairs here. She first pretended interest in the World War II exhibit in the niche off the first landing, but soon found her interest genuinely taken by the descriptions alongside the old black and white photos.

German U-boats in Conception Bay? Who would have thought? The submarines had been targeting ships laden with iron ore mined from deep below the ocean on Bell Island, right across the tickle from her own home. And successfully. At least three ships had been taken down over the span of a couple of months in '42, with a large loss of life. This was getting interesting. There'd never been any attacks on land from the Germans, though a 'friendly fire' had smashed into an area north of Portugal Cove, the exhibit told her. The thought crossed her mind that this must have been close to St. Jude Without.

Her breath recovered, she continued on her way. It had been a hard winter with little physical activity, and Carmel was way too out of shape. She was going to have to get fitter than this.

She was in the public room of the archives, checking out references on early editions of newspapers on the microfilm when the old map was delivered. There was little ceremony in it; a courier dropped it off to the eager hands of Marcia Flynn, the head archivist, who quickly tore open the stiff envelope to examine the old paper. Tina, the front desk clerk, stood on tippy-toes behind her, peering past the frizzy hair to see what the map held, but Marcia must have felt her hot breath down her neck for the archivist turned and glared at the young woman, then scuttled away to the back rooms without sharing the map with a soul. Carmel would have to find a chance later in the day to ask to have a look at it.

Tidying her papers after she finished her research, Carmel stood up from the desk and as she did, her eye was caught by the dirty red of a familiar plaid jacket. Nate O'Reilly again! Ugh, three times she'd seen him now in less than twenty-four hours. He looked to be flirting with Tina, the front desk clerk, but she could see he was actually watching everything that went on in the large public room. Carmel turned her back on him and pretended she hadn't seen him, and quickly slipped out of the room.

"Whoah, there!"

She'd been so intent on not acknowledging Nate that she hadn't looked to see where she was going, and almost banged into David as she came out into the mezzanine opening out over the huge building.

"Sorry about that," she said. 'I wasn't uh, paying attention."

"On your way to coffee break? Let's go up to the restaurant."

The top floor restaurant of The Rooms was far nicer than the usual airless staff lounge on the main floor, except that the coffee wasn't free up there. They sat at a window table looking out over the city, the old downtown spread below with the harbor and Signal Hill framing the view. With their backs to the room, this setting had an unexpected intimacy with a bird's eye view of the bustling streets far below.

David encouraged her to talk about herself, and she was flattered by the eye contact he now bestowed on her, short glances only as if he was fearful of unleashing the whole of his charisma. He's shy, she found herself thinking. Not making eye contact is a protective mechanism he's learned to put into place.

Likewise, she in turn encouraged him to talk about himself, for he was still a mysterious figure she wanted to know more about. His Master's specialty research topic had been a history of his family's business and how their prominence had helped shape the province under colonial rule in their placement in government, business and church. He'd used primary sources from his father's attic, documents that had been hoarded away until he brought them to light, everything from shipping bills to personal diaries.

"They didn't throw anything away, I swear," he said, laughing. "Two hundred and fifty years of history were stored in that old attic."

"So there you are!" A bright voice cut through the cozy atmosphere of their chat. Tina plopped herself down across from Carmel with a relieved smile, her mousy brown hair tied back into a simple ponytail and her huge glasses perched on the end of her small nose. "I was looking everywhere." She looked all around her. "Nice place they got here. Sort of expensive, though, isn't it?"

"What's up?" Carmel asked her. "Was there something special you needed?"

"No," replied Tina, with a wide smile. "Just thought I'd come to coffee with you guys for a change."

"Oh," Carmel said after a tiny pause. David was not speaking a word--she could almost feel him withdrawing back into his shell. "That's nice."

A short silence followed, during which Tina looked at the two of them expectantly as if waiting to be entertained.

Carmel turned back to David for she'd been enjoying their talk and didn't see why they had to stop midway through to include Tina. "So I guess you're interested in the map they found beneath Water Street then," Carmel said, "in your family's old business premises."

"Map?" David looked up from his examination of his cup and stared at her.

He hadn't heard the news, so she filled him in on what Darrow had told her. Tina didn't interrupt again, seeming happy enough to sit and listen, her head bobbing back and forth as if she were at a tennis match.

"I've read about an early Clerkwell connection with St. Jude Without," he said, nodding slowly. "There's mention in the diaries."

"I guess the chest belonged to your family. Do you think they'd want to claim it?"

"If, as you say, it's just full of old rags, then probably not," he replied, a smile on his face. "Especially if it comes with an unexplained murder victim. Best not go there."

She purposefully held back on Phonse's version of the map's history. It didn't paint David's illustrious ancestors in a very good light, especially with the skeleton as proof the story might be true.

"I think the map is just a scrap," she confided, but then she saw her chance to have a look at the map and perhaps get a copy for Phonse. "It's not really a map at all, Darrow said. But why don't you ask Marcia for a look at it? I wouldn't mind seeing it, too."

"That might be difficult," he said, after a pause.

"It arrived this morning––I saw Marcia accept it," Carmel said.

Tina nodded vigorously in agreement. "But she won't let you see it, I'll tell you that now. She wouldn't even let me look at it," she said as she took off her glasses to clean them.

Without the heavy spectacles, Carmel could see her eyes were a soft gray. Glancing back at David, she caught herself in surprise.

"You guys have the same eyes. I never noticed be-fore. Are you related?" It was true––their eyes were the same silvery gray, yet this wasn't obvious at first glance for David's were outlined with lush dark lashes, which Carmel thought were criminally wasted on a man. Tina's light lashes and brows caused the same gray to fade away in a washed-out anonymity.

David's coffee paused in mid-air as he stiffened.

"There might be a family connection," Tina said as she glanced slyly over at David, smiling a little at his discomfort.

"The only connection would be by pure chance," David said in a low voice. "Stray dogs don't have family trees."

At this odd pronouncement, Tina recoiled as if struck. Her mouth set into a firm line and she gave Carmel a tight smile. "I'd better go," she said, looking at the clock on the wall. "Not everyone is entitled to take half hour coffee breaks."

"What was that all about?" Carmel asked David, watching Tina leave the restaurant, although she wasn't sure she really wanted to know.

He flicked his hand dismissively. "Never mind that," he said, "but let me tell you something about Marcia."

David leaned in towards her. "Like many academics, Marcia is a hoarder. They're a strange breed, so jealous of every little thing, they can't stand to think of anyone stepping in their territory. A lot of insecurity in these circles, you know. Everyone needs to be the most expert in their field, otherwise they've outlived their usefulness. It's a strange world, academia."

"You seemed to have escaped that neuroticism," Carmel pointed out. "You seem pretty normal." And it was true, despite what his cousin Rhonda had said about him.

"Ah, but I'm not at the top of the heap, am I?" His eyes danced a little in fun as he said this. "I've got nothing to lose yet."

Chapter 6

After the coffee break was finished, they passed through the public room of the archives. It was busy as usual with a handful of visitors looking to trace genealogical lines, along with a smattering of MUN students doing last minute research for papers due yesterday, and amateur historians searching for treasures. Nate was nowhere to be seen.

David nudged Carmel and pointed out Dr. Tony Taverstock, a large man arguing with Tina about the location of a vital paper from 1934 which was nowhere to be found. He wore a grayish smock unbuttoned over his shirt and suspenders, and carried a bulky down winter jacket over one arm as he expostulated with the other. As wide around as he was tall, he looked like a male version of Marcia with his fluffy hair, thick wire-rimmed glasses and mismatched clothing, except his chosen palette was in the dun-colored range. He was the head of the university library, and as the keeper of all knowledge in that institution considered himself welcome wherever he chose to go.

"Speaking of neurotic academics..." David drew Carmel aside and spoke in her ear. "Marcia and Tony have been at loggerheads for the past twenty years. The fights between those two are the stuff of legends. They each claim the other is withholding valuable documents and squashing academic freedom. It's a case of the pot calling the kettle black, really."

"I know the exact location of the Squires file!" Tony yelled at Tina as he loomed his large bulk over her. "Just because you didn't put it back in the right place doesn't mean it's not there. Just let me in there, I'll find it!" He gave an exasperated huff. "Where's Marcia when you need her?"

"She's not answering her phone; I think she might be down in the basement archives somewhere. But I can't allow you to go back there, sir," she said desperately. "It's for staff only."

"What's the trouble, Tony?" David asked as he approached the pair.

"They've lost the blasted Squires' portfolio," the professor told him. "This wouldn't happen in my camp."

"I'm sure it's not lost," David said smoothly. "Didn't you have that out last week?"

"So it should be there!" Tony crowed with triumph.

"Well, we don't usually allow visitors in the backrooms as you know," David said, "but someone of your eminence can surely be trusted." He flashed a glance at the large man who immediately relaxed, mollified. "Tina's pretty busy at the desk here. You know your way around?"

"I know this place like my own library," Tony replied. "I helped design the Archives layout, if you remember." He puffed his chest out and strode through the gate, waiting impatiently for the clerk to swipe him access to the back.

"Take all the time you need, Tony," David said with a serene smile and a gleam in his eye.

Carmel saw her opportunity. Marcia was down in the basement, and she could nip down there now and ask her for a look at the map, maybe even snag a photocopy of it for Phonse. Although why she was bothering, Carmel wasn't sure, for Darrow had assured her there was little on the map itself except for the outline of the cove of St. Jude without. Still, she'd promised Phonse and he'd been pretty insistent that she do this for him. It would only take a moment.

"I just have to go down to the basement for a moment," she told David. "I won't be long."

He frowned distractedly. "Right now?" He glanced at his watch. It was a fancy expensive looking one, gleaming gold even under the fluorescent lights. He gave a small pout. "Can you hurry up with that, then? I need you to sort that filing on my desk before lunch."

"You know I won't be hanging out down there longer than I need to," she said with a smile she didn't feel.

Because there was just one slight problem with her plan. The basement archives. OMG. Carmel had a phobia of dark places, especially those underground. The room she was intending to go to was deep below this massive building, with long corridors of stacks looming fifteen feet into the air. It was a place where the lights were on timers and were movement sensitive, where if you didn't find what you needed quickly, you could be plunged into deepest black with no way out.

On her tour of the building, the first day of work, David had taken her down to the archive room. Noticing her hesitancy in entering the basement, he had turned his lovely eyes on her and she'd found herself breaking down, confessing the claustrophobia which had haunted her ever since she was a young girl, left with the Sisters by a mother who preferred to travel the world than tend to her only child. The Sisters had been a kindly group of women except for Sister Oliphant who'd had a habit of locking young children in the cupboard under the stairs for the most minor of misdeeds and filling their heads with tales of the darbies and other nasties who lurked in dark spaces and ate bad children.

He had assured her the basement was safe and had been kind in his very thorough explanation of the lighting system. "The lights will turn off if they don't sense movement within a period of time," he said. "But the rare time that happens, all you need to do is move––take a step, flap your arms, anything at all––the motion sensors are everywhere. You'll never be down here for that long though, because everything is catalogued with the numbering system and easy to find.

"Just one thing. Never, ever turn the light switch off when you're leaving," he had cautioned. "They'll go out automatically. That makes it easier on the next person to come in––they won't have to feel around looking for the light switch."

He had brought her into the long room filled with what seemed like miles of shelving drawers, and he'd pointed out the doorstop. "To further ease your mind," he said. "Don't be embarrassed to use the dog to wedge the door open. You're not the only one who hates the dark."

The dog he spoke of was a statue in the shape of a Newfoundland dog, about a foot long and eight inches high, standing guard outside the door. It was a friendly looking fellow, as most Newfoundland dogs are, with a patina of rust all over the cast iron sculpture.

Carmel was a grown-up now, but the five year old girl still quivered inside her and was petrified to go alone into that basement. She had successfully avoided it until this moment.

Tina accosted her with a list before she got through the door. "If you're going down there, would you mind picking these up for me?"

So much for her quick visit in and out of the basement archive room, but there was no helping that, she couldn't say no to the woman's very reasonable request. And at least that meant Tina wouldn't be down there and Carmel was more likely to be alone with Marcia in the room. Asking for a copy of an as-yet undocumented paper was probably taboo in the archivist's world, and if there was an audience, Marcia was likely to act the drama queen and pull rank in a loud refusal. She might be more amenable if there was just the two of them.

Despite David's urging for haste, Carmel was in no rush to force herself down there, but finally there was no escaping it. She had to brave the depths, so to make it as painless as possible, she avoided the closed-in elevator and took the back stairs down the numerous stairs. She found herself finally in the basement corridor of doors, most of them leading to utility closets, electrical rooms and the like, with the archive room at the end around the last corner. But one was marked with the universal sign indicating it was a toilet and she could put off the evil for a moment at least, perhaps five minutes. Sometimes the five-year-old girl within also controlled her bladder.

Carmel sighed with relief to see the door to the archive room already propped open with the antique iron dog statue which kept the door firmly in place––at least if the worst happened she would still have the florescent lights from the corridor flooding into the stacks.

And Marcia was right there at the front of the room by the shelves just ten feet inside the doorway. The archivist was searching through files and boxes, taking papers out and making quite a mess on the table behind her. As she approached, Carmel glanced down at the various documents spread out, and there was the very map, now carefully protected in a see-through Mylar envelope. She stretched her neck for a closer look, but the movement caught the head archivist's attention, and she glared at the younger woman for disturbing her domain.

'Hi, Dr. Flynn," Carmel began, her voice bright and friendly. "That must be the map that was found in the cellar on the old Clerkwell property..." But that was as far as she got before Marcia humphed at her.

"I was wondering if..." she began again in a faltering voice but to no avail.

"Don't bother me now," Marcia cut in. She took up the open file with the map and closed it so it was hidden. She clutched it to her chest as she looked at Carmel with an accusation in her eye before turning her back on her altogether.

That hadn't gone well. Carmel looked down at the list of files Tina had given her. There was nothing to do but to go look for them since she was down here anyway. Of course, they were located at the back of the cavernous room, but at least Marcia was another living human being down here in the depths, someone who would keep away the ghouls and trolls who lived in the dark of her imagination. She didn't have to be friendly, just alive. Marcia was also moving around enough to keep the motion sensors occupied and the lights on full.

The file numbers led her right to the back of the long stacks, several shelves in, to the point furthest from the door. Fortunately, the archives were kept in impeccable order so she would be able to track the necessary documents quickly and run out of the basement again.

Only, it was never that easy, of course. The filing was according to number and letter sequences, and when she was nervous she had to repeat the whole alphabet song in her head, especially for anything after L-M-N-O-P. She had at last found the first of the file folders when she heard a muffled voice through the stacks.

"What are you doing?" It was Marcia, indignant over something. She could have been calling out to Carmel, or she could have been speaking in her normal tone to someone standing next to her.

"I'm way down here at the back, Marcia," she called back, to be on the safe side. "Do you need anything?"

She received no answer. Perhaps her voice had got swallowed up in the vastness of the room with its never ending stacks, and the ventilation system with its fans and motors creating a barrier of white noise. Better go see what the boss wanted. Carmel turned to go back the way she had come.

She heard Marcia again, muffled this time, and almost thought a voice answered her. But then a loud piercing shriek sounded through the stacks, cut off by a thump and the room went pitch black. Before her eyes could adjust to the change, she heard the muffled thump of the door to the corridor as it closed.

Black. Much blacker even than under the stairs in the convent all those years ago. Not even the soft red light of the fire escape sign to light her way. The room grew inexplicably cold as the scream echoed in her ears.

Chapter 7

C armel couldn't move, didn't dare move for fear of losing her sense of direction in this space which had had all the light sucked out of it with the suddenness of a power outage. The blackness was a solid mass encasing her like a coffin. She heard a whimper of fear as she reached out for the bookcase which had been in front of her just a moment ago, and it wasn't till she touched the cold metal that she realized the sound had come from her own throat. She was totally alone down here now.

She had to get out, but knew she couldn't let the panic take her or she might be wandering for days within this vast echoey place. She flapped her arms as instructed by David, but the movements weren't setting off the motion sensors––somewhere at the back of her mind was a memory of his explanation that they only worked if there was a source of power, in other words if the light switch was physically on. Either the power was out or someone had turned off the switch before they'd shut the door. Deliberately.

"Hello?" she called out. There was no answer. And where was Marcia?

Carmel crept her way back from where she'd come until she reached the break in the shelves. Was it left or right to the far wall? Carmel had to stop to take deep breaths in order to still the panic which was threatening to bubble over. She hated being so blind in this unknown space, and by now the blood was pounding in her head like an alarm. Or was it an alarm that she in fact was hearing? She would have cause to remember that afterwards.

She stretched out with both arms as she made her way back along the wall, counting the shelving units on her left until they reached an abrupt end and her hand was left dangling in space.

"Marcia?" she whispered, for she thought she was where the archivist had last been. There was only the white noise of the ventilation system, her own breathing, and an endless harsh bleating pulsation far away.

At last, her hand touched the wood of the table where Marcia had been stacking her finds. Carmel grasped it in both hands like a long lost friend, knocking some files to the floor as she did so. "Oh, thank God," she said, allowing herself to breathe again. "Marcia, are you here? The door should be just over..." But her hands which had been freezing were now warm, a wet warm, and she realized the new texture beneath her fingers was hair.

"Marcia?" she said with doubt in her voice.

It was all so sudden what happened next––the door bursting open and the alarm so much louder that it seemed to be on top of her, the lights flashing on, then David's look of horror at the sight of her with blood on her hands and his scream echoing her own. She looked down at her hands and saw the blood and a skull smashed open and her screams went on and on. David turned and fled, leaving her alone in the harsh light with Marcia's body.

***

When Darrow found her, she was curled up against the stacks hyperventilating, her hands held out in front of her and their red cover slowly congealing to an un-speakable dark brick. David had been mistaken about the timing. It had been a full ten minutes and she hadn't moved and the lights were still glaring down at her.

Inspector Darrow stood by and allowed his team to fall into action like a smoothly oiled machine. He and a female officer approached her quietly, and he removed his winter coat and placed it around her shoulders.

Evelyn Wright, his partner, shot him a sharp glance which he quelled with one of his own. "She's in shock," he told her.

He turned to the mess that had been Carmel. "Look at me," he ordered her, not unkindly. "What happened?"

She was shivering by now, and could only hold onto the warm brown concern in his eyes like a lifeline. She heard his voice ask the questions, but couldn't make the connection inside her head that she should be answering.

He sighed and looked at Evelyn, standing by, armed with handcuffs.

"No," he said with a force that surprised even himself. "She's not fit... Damnit, it can't be as it looks. Find a quiet space for her, one with a view of the daylight, and a strong cup of sweet tea." He knew about her claustrophobic tendencies.

"And Evelyn," he added, "be gentle."

So Carmel found herself in a quiet room, a left-over space used to store worn-out armchairs, gulping in the sight of blue sky and bare March trees and a view of the Basilica across the road. The warmth of the cup in her hands helped bring her back. They were clean again. Evelyn had with due diligence taken swabs and then scrubbed her hands for her as if she were a child. Another constable sat out of sight, notebook in hand.

She shifted uncomfortably in the clothing which had been scrounged up for her from the lost and found box and from disused staff lockers. So humiliating to be asked to remove all her clothing––yes, all of it, even her bra and underwear. She blessed her own vanity for wearing a matching set of lacies, but she hoped they would be returned at some point. This set wasn't from the boutique lingerie shop on Water Street, just standard mall issue, but they still didn't come cheap.

The sweat pants were loose, while the socks didn't feel overly clean. And the sneakers were two sizes too big and smelled bad. The huge green hoody was at least warm and covered the fact that she no longer had a bra to wear.

"What happened?" Evelyn's voice was soft as she sat across Carmel, elbows on her knees and hands dangling in an unthreatening way.

Carmel tried to pull herself together. "I had to go down there, for the files... for Tina. I had it all figured out, could just run down there, find them, run back out again because of the ..."

"The dark?"

She nodded and took a sip of tea. "The lights went out and there was a scream..."

"Are you sure of that sequence of events?"

Carmel's eyes looked up to the left then right, searching her memory. "No, yes... I'm not sure. Sorry. I mean, Marcia asked me something, and I called back, then the lights went out.

"It all happened so quickly," she continued. She let out a deep breath, then looked at her hands again and shivered. "The blood..."

"Your hands are clean now," Evelyn reassured her.

"I know, but I can still feel it... so warm and then afterwards, so sticky..."

"I need you to concentrate on my questions," Evelyn's voice was firm, directing her back to the here and now. "What happened between the time that you found Dr. Flynn's body and David opening the door?"

"Nothing; it seemed to happen at the same time," she answered. "I found the table, sent something flying, but I was so relieved I didn't care. Then my hands were....

And then the door opened and that noise was so loud and the lights came on and David was screaming. And I was, too, I guess."

Evelyn nodded then stood up. "Okay. I want you to sit here a while. Inspector Darrow will no doubt want to speak with you himself. Meanwhile, if you remember anything, or need anything, Constable Brown will be right here with you."

Carmel looked behind her and saw the young woman in uniform. She didn't look over eighteen years old, but she wore a kindly expression in her earnest and intelligent blue eyes.

"Constable Wright?"

"It's Sergeant now," Evelyn replied, correcting her.

A promotion, then. Surely well deserved. "How's David?"

Evelyn caught her breath. "He's well. Well as can be expected."

"Can I see him?"

The policewoman paused before answering. "No, that wouldn't be advisable right now." She didn't say it, but Carmel could see it in the way her eyes averted.

"Does he think I did it? That I killed Dr. Flynn?"

Evelyn didn't deny it but went on her way.

***

"You don't think I killed her, do you?" Carmel was quickly recovering from the shock of the morning now that she had Darrow's presence by her side again.

"I have serious doubts as to the likelihood of that," he said firmly. He glanced over at the young constable, who was sitting very straight on the edge of her seat with her face forward, so new to her job that she was terrified of this man, her boss. His hand worked its way through his silver laced hair, making it stand up on end.

Carmel ached to smooth it down for him but held back.

"Constable Brown, can I trouble you to find me a cup of coffee?" he asked. "Milk, not cream. There should be a pot in the staff room along the corridor."

He turned to her as soon as Brown had left.

"Of course, I don't think you killed Marcia Flynn," he hissed through his teeth. "But you have to stop doing this."

That was so unfair.

"You think I go looking for bodies to stumble over?" She couldn't believe what she was hearing. They glared at each other, blue eye on brown, until a noise from the corridor brought them back to their senses.

"Sorry. I know you don't," he said, looking away. "But I wish you wouldn't. I worry for you.

"And this one is frustrating," he continued in a low voice. "We both know you had no reason to do this, but it doesn't look good. You know we canna see each other until this is over."

"You're seriously worrying about that when there's a killer on the loose?" She didn't bother keeping her voice low. Honest to God, she had thought this guy was different, but he was as selfish as Phonse, thinking only of himself at all times.

He looked at her again, puzzlement in his eyes at her tone until a light of understanding broke through.

"I meet with killers every month. We'll find whoever did this," he said. "Relationships––now they're much more rare." His voice became sombre again. "Are you worried? Do you think you're in danger?"

"You mean.... It could have been me that got killed," she said slowly as the realization hit her for the first time. "Oh God, I hadn't thought about that. But I didn't witness anything. Did I?" She knew she wasn't making sense, but she couldn't stop. "Why would someone kill Marcia?"

"For the life of me, I can't answer that one," he admitted. "Professional jealousy? Find the motive, and you'll find the murderer, as they say."

"I have to ask," Carmel hesitated. "But how did she die? From what I've seen of the archives, there's only paper and books there. I didn't hear a gun shot or anything to account for all that blood."

"The one thing that could have killed her was used," Darrow answered. "She was hit on the side of her head with the Newfoundland dog doorstop. It's a solid iron creature from the Victorian era."

The one thing available to kill her with was the one lifeline that had had enabled Carmel to feel okay about entering the cavernous basement in the first place, the thing which ensured her of light by keeping the door open. Yet it had taken Marcia's lights out.

He looked like he had more to say but was not given the chance. Darrow straightened and cleared his throat as soon as he heard Constable Brown's light foot on the linoleum outside the room, coffee in hand. "Well, thank you for your assistance," he said to Carmel. "Sergeant Wright will return shortly to take your statement. Good-bye, Ms. McAlistair."

That was the last she was to see of John Darrow that day.

It was a while before Sergeant Wright came to take her statement and while she waited, she could overhear the interviews happening across the hall if she concentrated hard enough. Tina, the desk clerk, was especially loud, being overwrought and excited by the drama.

"Well, I wasn't on the desk the whole time, no," she said plaintively. "How could I be? I have to go back and forth all the time. They expect me to be everywhere at once."

"No, I didn't see anyone suspicious at all," she continued. "There was no one coming out with blood all over them, if that's what you mean. Not that I saw, anyway."

A low mumble as the officer asked her a question.

"Yes, I heard the alarm, but didn't think anything of it," she said. "There's always staff going out of the fire doors in the building––they just can't be bothered coming back up all these stairs and going down again to the main entrance. If I had to panic every time I heard an alarm I'd never get anything done here."

The police officer must have spoken again.

"Everyone is all over the place," Tina said, her high voice tinged with exasperation. "I'm too busy to keep an eye on what they're all doing."

Another pause, then Tina spoke again. "I was in the back rooms, filing. When I was coming back, Dr. Taverstock almost knocked me over when he left. That was a minute or two before David came running in, screaming and throwing up. Maybe longer, I don't know," she said. "Dr. T. was in his usual tearing rush; he had his overcoat on already and he just pushed past me and left without a thank-you or anything. But there was nothing out of the ordinary, no."

Sergeant Wright entered the room at that moment and closed the door. She took a brief statement from Carmel. Despite the evidence to the contrary, Darrow didn't have her charged with the murder and Carmel was quickly sent home to recover. She asked when she should return to her job, but received no answer, just the archival equivalent of 'don't call us, we'll call you.'

Chapter 8

"So looks like I've lost my job out of it," she said into her beer at the bar that evening.

"They're not going to fire you if you didn't kill Dr. Flynn," Phonse said. He didn't have much of a grasp on corporate culture, having never participated in it.

"I'm pretty sure that's against union rules," Bridget added, "though, of course, you're probably still in your probationary period, in which case you haven't got a leg to stand on. They can find any reason not to have you back."

"Thanks, Bridget. You're a real comfort."

"We all knew no good would come of this." This came from Phonse.

"Murder is pretty awful, yeah," Carmel agreed. "I guess they still think I'm guilty, even though the police didn't arrest me for it. Yet."

"No, I mean the chest, of course."

"That old wooden chest? What's that got to do with anything? Phonse, there was nothing inside that except old clothes," Carmel reminded him. She intercepted a look between the two. "And the map."

"Did you get it for me?"

"Phonse, have you been listening? I just found a body in the most gruesome possible way. I have other things on my mind than your stupid map."

"Did you even see the map?"

"Yes, she had it down in the basement when I saw her..."

"And you didn't take it? I mean, after she was dead, she didn't need it anyway, did she?"

Carmel could only stare at him. Was he mad? "I couldn't... I mean, I was in shock... No, I didn't take the map from her! I'd quite forgotten about your dumb map by then, Phonse."

Phonse looked at her levelly. "Look, Carmel, I understand you've been through a horrible experience," he said. "But I need you to understand that we have to have this map. A lot is riding on it."

"But there's nothing on the map..." she began.

"How do you know that?"

"Darrow said so," she told him, after a short pause.

"And you trust what he said? A cop? What does he know?" Phonse crossed his arms. "He wouldn't be able to read the map like we could. I'm counting on you to get a hold of that map."

She sighed. "I've been fired; remember?"

"Well, you're just going to have to un-fire yourself, missy," Phonse said, poking his finger in her shoulder as he stood up. "We need you. You'll figure it out, you're a smart girl."

"That's right," nodded Bridget. "This must be the whole reason Jem allowed you into the cove. You're the one to return Eliza's dowry to his descendants."

Captain Jem's ghost, they meant, of course. They weren't sane, surely. The two cousins stared at her as if expecting her to turn right around and go back to town to pick up the map. "We're counting on you," Phonse said. "And remember, this is a surprise for Nate, so don't let on to him."

***

The next day, the bomb scares began. Unaware of this development, Darrow was called into Chief Inspector Yvonne Hender's office at 9:05 a.m. It was a meeting he'd been about to propose himself after a long conflicted night of little sleep.

"I'm glad to have this opportunity," Darrow informed her on entering her office and taking the seat she'd indicated. Her office was on the floor above his, with the same view of the South Side hills but being that much higher, the morning sun slanted in unfettered by the shadow of The Rooms. "I need to take myself off the Flynn murder case."

Hender sat back in her plush chair and regarded him steadily, her clear eyes focused and seeing the hard night he'd passed.

"I concur," she said in a voice as crisp as her white blouse and the sharp cut of her silver hair. "What were you thinking? I expect better of you, of all my officers. I couldn't believe it when they told me."

He nodded, elbows resting on his knees and hands clasped. She was waiting for a full explanation.

"I know the woman who was found by the victim's side," he said. That in itself wasn't so rare in this small city, for one had to be friendly with neighbors and others one might meet in the run of the day. It was the emotional connection with Carmel that was the issue. Hender was already aware of this, yet he knew she would require him to lay out the details and give a full confession to show he fully understood the grievous mistake he'd made the previous day.

"And the rumors are correct that she's your girl-friend?"

"No, no," Darrow denied, with a shake of his head. "However, I don't deny there are possibilities there."

"And you didn't think to call in for someone else to step in right away?"

"That's correct," he confessed after a pause. This was not easy for him. "I wasn't thinking. I was acting on misguided instinct. I allowed my emotions to get the better of me."

"You realize you may have already caused irreparable harm to the investigation?"

He winced, but he would have done the same to someone under his command in the same situation. Had done, in fact. "Yes, I am fully aware. By not removing myself and allowing another officer to take charge, I may have allowed vital evidence to escape detection. By attempting to protect Ms. McAlistair, I may have allowed the actual perpetrator to remain undiscovered."

He could feel her stare burning into him, so lifted his eyes to meet her.

"And?"

"The evidence points to her as the perpetrator," he said reluctantly, "but..."

"No buts," she said curtly. "I've assigned another officer to the case. Also, we just received a report of a bomb threat at the Confederation Building. I'm putting you in charge of that."

He sat up quickly, his back rigid in protest. A mere bomb scare? Those were a dime a dozen, regular monthly occurrences. This was a harsh punishment, surely, a huge demotion in duties. Hender was pulling rank and showing him, and everyone else at the RNC, who was the boss. Darrow swallowed the quick burst of anger that rose in his throat.

"Standard operating procedures in place?"

"Yes," she replied. Seeing his acceptance of the assignment without verbal protest, Hender finally relaxed a bit in her chair. "Perfect timing; they waited until all the bureaucrats were in the government offices before calling it, thus achieving the maximum disruption."

"How was the notification made?"

"An on-air call to the morning radio show," she noted. "Creating a huge panic in the population, of course." She looked up at him with a small grin. "So I'm glad to have you on board with that. It's not so routine, after all, you'll be happy to hear."

"Any suspicions as to who made the call?"

She shook her head. "The voice wasn't recognizable, could barely make out the words. And probably used a throw away phone, so it'll be untraceable from that aspect. I suspect the NLA."

Darrow allowed himself a small chuckle. "The Newfoundland Liberation Army. I've noticed an upsurge of the posters on the lightpoles."

"And t-shirts too, this time round," Hender noted. "You'd almost think it was an organized effort."

Every decade or so a similar thing happened. A new generation of youth with too much time on their hands, a lack of purpose but with romantic dreams would latch onto the idea that independence from the mother country would be the solution to their woes. An underground movement would be launched, an upswell from this disenfranchised group which would last at least until the hot weather cooled and the youth had to enter the regular life of jobs and paying back student loans.

"Anyway, that's something to get your teeth into," she said. "And I don't need to tell you––hands off the Flynn case. Although if you see McAlistair around, I want her brought in for questions."

"For questioning only?"

Hender hesitated, considering the question seriously. "An arrest wouldn't be out of the question. Given the evidence we have." She locked eyes with Darrow and dared him to deny the proof of the scant evidence collected so far, and his part in that lack.

Once again he swallowed his words and nodded professionally before taking his leave.

Chapter 9

It was ridiculous to think of, really. Carmel was fuming. Here she was, the number one suspect for killing the woman who held the map, and her friends were requesting she go back to the scene of the murder and retrieve it.

As if it would be that easy. First off, she'd have to beg for her job back from David in order to gain entrance into the back rooms of the archives for, as the next in line to Marcia, he would be acting head till they found a replacement for her. Remembering the horror on his face as he looked at her over Dr. Flynn's body, she didn't think she'd have much luck with that. He thought she was a murderer.

Even if she could worm her way back into his good graces, she'd have to get her hands on the map, or at least a copy of it. It might take weeks, maybe months or years, before it was catalogued and put into circulation. After all, everyone thought it was a useless scribble. Even Darrow had said it was just a scrap of paper.

But Marcia hadn't thought so. The map had been lying on the table next to the archivist as she feverishly combed through the shelf of archives before her life had been cut short. It may even have been ruined with her blood. Mylar film was used to store old documents instead of plastic as it was acid-free, she knew, but was it as protective as plastic? Would it be permeable to blood? Was it one of the files she had knocked to the floor before her hands found Marcia's blood? She had no way of knowing.

The stupid map might even be held as part of evidence in the search for Marcia's murderer. Only Darrow could answer that question for her, and it really looked like Darrow wouldn't be in contact in the near future.

All this thinking helped keep at bay the horrors of the day before, but it wasn't enough. She needed to go for a long walk to clear her head, preferably not anywhere near her home. St. Jude Without held too many memories of murders and death in the short time she'd lived there, too many reminders of horror, and Phonse's insensitivity was not helping matters at all. She had to get away from them, and away from Marcia's death. Carmel needed a mindless walk in a cool wind to calm her thoughts.

She'd meant to head for her familiar walk around Quidi Vidi Lake but after she drove all the way there and parked her car, she found the paths were still treacherous with ice. Instead, she walked up the slight slope of Kings Bridge Road and then downhill again towards the harbor. Her steps unconsciously took her to the place where it all began.

The old Clerkwell premises were unrecognizable by now. What had been a deserted grassy field of rubble and stone and iron pipes on the water's edge in the heart of the city's downtown was now a true construction site of earth movers, cranes and port-a-potties. She leaned against the iron fence surrounding the harbor and looked back at the site, feeling the cold metal at her back.

Iron. Like the iron which had killed Marcia.

Turning, she watched as a couple of young teenagers walked by with a large toffee-colored Newfoundland dog. The girl's dancing brown eyes reminded her of someone she knew; she had a familiar look to her that Carmel couldn't place, but the dog with that coloring looked just like the rusty sculpture that had taken the head archivist's life. Carmel couldn't get away from the reminders today.

The dog snuffled at her in passing and smelt her hand. She attempted to give him a scratch under the chin only to come away with a handful of drool.

"Irn!" she heard the girl say as she tugged on the leash. "Come away. Sorry, miss, he's a really nosy dog."

"S'okay," said Carmel, wiping her hand on her jeans as she turned to make her way back up towards Water Street.

Just under the courthouse steps, she was accosted by a food vendor, a rare sight in a Newfoundland March. Even on a sunny warmish day like this.

"A deep-fried pirogue for a beautiful lady?" The man leaned out of the window of the small van pulled up into the parking lot. Her heart sank for she knew that heavily accented voice. Not now, not on top of everything else. His hard green eyes belied the playful tone of his voice.

"Ruscan." Her one-time lover, the Ukrainian she had met in South-east Asia on her travels, all those years ago. He had disappeared from an airplane midflight over Taiwan leaving her to mourn him as dead, and then he'd followed her all the way across the world, but something had happened to him in between. He was why she had left Darrow during their date on New Year's Eve. He had texted her and like a fool she had followed. She'd had to discover the truth.

And she had. Ruscan Milanovic was a changed man from the one she thought she'd known. She could well believe now that he had been mixed up in some sort of international mafia group as people had said. If she could have had her time back...

He had taken her rejection well, but having no means of leaving the island, he'd stuck around as the only way off the island was an expensive plane flight or an equally costly ferry-ride to Nova Scotia. The iron fence surrounding the working part of the harbor precluded his stowing away on board a cargo ship. The last she'd heard, he was squatting in the rusted Lyubov Orlova at the far end of the harbor and had applied for refugee status.

She looked up at him. "You have a job?"

"This, no!" he said. "I'm looking after this for a friend. He has other things to do right now, and needs me to help his business." He swept his arm around as if indicating hordes of people about to engulf him. The street was fairly empty at this time of day, half an hour before noon.

She didn't want to know. "Still squatting on that ship?"

"Eh," he was non-committal. "It's legal. I'm the night security guard. Every night I'm there. They pay me, and give me the electric also."

"You don't mind the rats?"

"The rats I have taken care of," he told her. "Care for a bowl of borscht?" Ruscan grinned evilly as he said this.

"No," she said quickly. "Definitely not. Why does your friend see the need to open the van in March? There's no-one around."

He leaned out of the window and tapped the side of his nose. "Watching, Carmel," he said. "We are always watching."

Dear God. How, how, how had she gotten mixed up with this nutcase, all those years ago? "Let me guess––aliens?"

"No," he disagreed with a total lack of humor. "Politics. The Newfoundland Independence movement. Just you wait––you will hear of us."

Oh great––a Ukranian national fighting for the freedom of Newfoundlanders. Just what they needed. "You're not involved with Nate, too, are you?" She couldn't keep the suspicion out of her voice.

"The least said about it the better," he whispered at her. "And your policeman, your tame piggie? How does he go?" There was definitely a hint of jealousy in his expression.

"He's not mine," she said, "and don't call him that."

"No?" he scowled. "Then why does he follow you around like one?" He pointed behind her, then the shutter of his van closed with a bang and two moments later the van scuttled down Water Street heading west, leaving a trail of exhaust in its wake.

Carmel turned and sure enough, there was Darrow standing at the opened passenger side door of an unmarked car, a thunderous look on his face.

"Does he have a license for that?" The Scots accent was thick in his voice today.

Carmel shrugged and walked towards him. "Who knows?"

"I don't trust that man," he continued. "He always looks guilty. I saw him yesterday morning at the Tim Horton's and even that early in the morning he looked like he was conspiring."

She looked at him, almost wanting to smile. Was that a tinge of jealousy in his voice?

"If it eases your mind any, he may be involved with the independence movement," she said. "So he's spending his energy with that lost cause and can't get into too much trouble."

He nodded curtly, as if he had other things on his mind. "I'm glad I found you. You're needed at the station," he said, indicating the car. Darrow had no choice but to obey his orders and bring her up to the station for questioning.

"Are you arresting me?" She was only half joking as she asked.

Really, she could understand it. Carmel had been caught with her hands full of blood, standing over Marcia's body, with no-one else in the vicinity. It still had an air of unreality about it for her. How likely was it that another person had snuck in, turned off the lights and used the door stop to bash Marcia's head in? And why would they do it?

She had heard another voice with Marcia, the lights went out and Marcia's scream, though, of course, she couldn't prove that. The archivist must have known her murderer when she saw him (or her) standing over her with the iron dog. Or did she?

"I'm not arresting you," he said as she drew next to him. "Against the advice of my own boss," he added softly. "We're taking you in for questioning," he said in a louder tone and opened the back door for her. She got in, the driver giving her a quick speculative glance before Darrow returned to the passenger seat.

The drive up Long's Hill to the police station was short, but seemed endless, and the red light at the top was the longest she'd ever experienced. Darrow looked straight ahead and spoke only with the constable at the wheel, isolating Carmel behind the steel netting. She had a sinking feeling in her gut. This treatment more than anything else so far was making her feel like a suspect. She wasn't even being granted the normal courtesy of an innocent member of the public, let alone one who had almost shared the intimacies of her bed with the man.

They entered the RNC building through a back entrance, a steel door which required a swipe card. She was taken to a room she'd never seen before, a far cry from Darrow's corner office with the comfortable visitor seating. This was a blank room, windowless and empty, the only personality was a smell of stale coffee and leftover sweat.

Sergeant Wright was waiting for them, her blond hair smoothed back into its severe bun. Her brow furrowed when Darrow spoke a word in her ear and she shot an unhappy look at Carmel, then she reluctantly left the room on whatever errand he had requested. The driver of the vehicle remained at the doorway.

Darrow remained at arm's length away from her. "You will need a lawyer present, Ms. McAlistair," he informed her. "For the questioning."

She stared at him as the horror of her situation dawned. He had said they couldn't see each other until the murder was solved, but was this formality really necessary? Darrow didn't appear to be on her side anymore.

"Lawyer? God, no," she squawked. "Do you really think I need one?"

"It would help," he replied, lowering his voice and his Scottish accent very evident. "It doesn't look good for you, and the higher ups are calling for blood."

It was worse than she thought, and getting worse all the time. Was he not going to help her at all? She had thought she could rely on his aid to get her through this.

"Look," he continued in a furious whisper, after he'd first glanced at the single constable by the door. His brown eyes were like flint––there was a lot at stake here. "I know you didn't murder her, but nobody else does. We've got to go by the book. I shouldn't even be here; I had to disclose our relationship and take myself off the case. I need you to help me with this."

A throat cleared at the doorway and he stepped away from her. "If you don't know or can't afford a lawyer," Wright began, "Miller from Legal Aid is in the building and is willing to act for you. You can get the paperwork done after."

"I don't need a lawyer," Carmel denied again. That would make the whole thing too real, having a lawyer would be like admitting a possibility of guilt.

A short stocky woman in a plaid shirt, blazer and jeans stepped out from behind Sergeant Wright. Her brush cut framed a face that was open and brooked no nonsense, and it was a familiar one.

"Carmel, you need a lawyer," Pam Miller told her in her flat voice.

"Pam!" Carmel exclaimed. "You're Pam from the Crisis Line last Christmas." The woman who had showed her the ropes at the phone line last year was brusque but gentle, a fighter for equality.

"And a Legal Aid lawyer," she replied, striding into the room and heaving a briefcase onto the laminated table. "I've heard the facts and believe me, honey, you do need me. Now, officers, I'd like some time with my client before you question her."

Carmel could have sworn she heard Darrow give a sigh of relief as the three members of the Constabulary left the room. She stared forlornly as he turned his back on her and, as far as she could see, washed his hands of her.

Chapter 10

After he'd left, Pam cocked her head in the direction of the door. "What's between you and the Inspector?"

"Nothing," Carmel said, too fast, remembering his caution to tell no-one of their relationship.

"Look, in order for this to work, I need you to tell me the truth in everything, Carmel, or else I can't help you," Pam said in her flat voice. "If it's nothing, why do you look like a puppy that just got kicked?"

Darrow had used the word 'disclosure.' A word with horrible connotations––so cold and clinical like she'd have to haul her heart out and lay it on the melamine table for dissection. Yet what she had with Darrow was still so fragile in its freshness, so green, she couldn't bear it.

"We've had a date," she mumbled, sitting on the orange plastic chair. "Or two. Nothing more. It's not like we've..."

"Exchanged bodily fluids?"

Carmel winced. "Please."

"Okay, so along with whatever has or hasn't happened between you and Inspector Darrow," said Pam, "I need you to tell me exactly what did happen the other day. Along with anything that might be relevant, including how you came to be working at The Archives in the first place."

It didn't take that long as there wasn't that much to tell, for she left out any mention of the map, pirates and St. Jude Without. That had nothing to do with Marcia's death, because that was just pure St. Jude Without craziness. Marcia just happened to be murdered while she was holding the stupid map.

"Hmm," said Pam after the tale was told. "Caught red-handed, steeped in her blood. Doesn't look good for you, does it?"

"No," Carmel replied, "when you put it that way, I guess it doesn't."

"So you and Darrow," Pam continued. "What do I need to know there?"

"That doesn't have anything to do with Marcia," Carmel insisted. "It's two people who like each other's company. A totally different storyline."

"Not when the media gets hold of it, as you're the prime suspect in the murder. And let's hope they don't get a whiff of this. I'm surprised he's still involved in the case. Not like him; he's usually very circumspect in his dealings."

"What is that supposed to mean?"

Pam caught her eye and gave a small laugh. "No, I don't mean he gets involved with potential murderers all the time. I've never even heard talk of him being one for the ladies except his ex-wife, and the justice community thrives on gossip." She paused for a moment in thought. "In fact, I distinctly remember a rumor that he batted for the home team, but that was probably just wishful thinking. Some guys like to think every good-looking man is gay."

"So where does this leave us?" Carmel interrupted. She didn't want to talk anymore about Darrow. "Am I going to be charged? Is that why they said I need you? They must think I did it. Have you ever represented a murderer before?"

"Once."

"How did that go?"

"He was convicted," Pam said. "But he was guilty. If it's any consolation, I really don't think you are."

"Thank you for that," Carmel said. She meant it.

"Ready for the questioning?"

Her blue eyes watered. "Do I have any choice?"

Pam looked at her, softening for the first time. "Look. A process has been set in motion, and all of the players––including you, me and the police––we have to follow through step by step. Just like if you were guilty––and I'm not saying you are. But if you were, you'd want all due diligence taken. Right?"

Carmel nodded.

"So it's the same thing when you're not guilty," Pam continued. "The police have to prove that they have examined every inch of the case before they can say they're certain you didn't do it. That puts everyone's mind at ease."

"Why didn't they do this right at the beginning then? Instead of letting me go home and hauling me in here the next day?" Carmel needed to know. "What's changed?"

Pam looked down at the tabletop in front of her and fiddled with her pen. "Um. Well, that's their problem. You don't need to worry about that right now. It shouldn't have any bearing on your case." She looked up with a smile pasted on her face. "It really shouldn't."

Sergeant Wright and a new officer filed into the room. She carried a jug of water and a stack of plastic cups.

"This is Inspector Laney," Evelyn said. Her expression was unreadable. "He's now in charge of the case." She sat down across the table.

Carmel drew in a breath to ask where Darrow was, but a sharp kick to her ankle shut her up. Pam looked at her and gave a quick shake of her head.

Laney still stood by his chair, arms crossed. Carmel could feel his eyes on her and glanced up. He was a heavy-set man with short close-cropped gray hair and a nose that had seen too much violence during his years on the force. Small eyes like rock chips and a mouth turned down at the corners by habit and life. He was old-school, all right. When she met his eyes, he gave a sniff, a snort that came from the back of his sinuses that managed to sound like a sneer. If he was trying to intimidate her it was working.

The sergeant gave the date and listed the room's occupants for the purpose of the recording device. And then it started.

Evelyn began the questioning and it was gentle at first. But when Carmel reached the point of her story that most upset her still even after numerous times recounting it, Laney stepped in.

"What were you using to cover your clothes?"

"I'm not sure I... what do you mean?"

"The blood sprayed back at you after the first hit," he said in his rough voice. "And the second. What were you using to stop the spray-back from getting all over you?"

"But I didn't use anything..."

"Don't lie to me. We already found your coverall stuffed away in the basement ladies room. It'll only be a matter of time before the results come back with evidence of your DNA on it."

She gaped at him. She had been in the toilet, or ladies room as he put it. Just before the murder. She had taken her time, reluctant to go into the vast archive storage room. Carmel had probably stood in front of the mirror and tried to find a semblance of order to her curls––she usually did whenever she caught sight of herself in a mirror.

So her DNA was probably all over that tiny room. If the murderer had thrown in a cover-all as he or she escaped the basement, well, they'd probably find her hair on it.

"Why did you leave the cloth bag on the scene?" he barked at her. "What angle did you hit her at then? Had it all figured out before hand, hey?"

"No, I didn't need ..."

"I agree, you didn't need anything. That was a nice touch, dipping your hands in the blood so it soaked up into your sleeves. Took care of that issue, didn't it?"

"Sergeant Laney, that's enough," barked Pam. "This is not an interrogation; my client is here assisting with questions."

His little eyes slid over to the lawyer and he said something under his breath.

"Your lips just moved, Sergeant Laney," Pam said clearly for the recorder. "Please repeat what you said for us all to hear."

Evelyn Wright sat there silently throughout it all with her arms crossed, taut as a tension wire caught both ways.

It must have gone on for more than an hour, this back and forth between Laney and herself, with frequent objections from Pam, but little from Darrow's partner Sergeant Wright. Later, Carmel had no idea what she'd said or admitted to, and could only trust in Pam's forthright presence beside her to guide her.

Until at last, Evelyn stood up abruptly. "This is getting us nowhere, Laney," she said. "We're rehashing the same old things. This interview is at an end." She switched off the recorder.

He stood up lazily and stretched his beefy arms. "I got better things to do with my time," he said. "Wasting it on a dyke and Darrow's piece of..."

"Enough," Evelyn cut in with a sharp voice. "Ms McAlistair, you're free to go for now. You may be required to return for further questioning. Please keep your cell-phone on and don't leave the greater St. John's area." Her face was paler than normal and there were lines around the corners of her eyes that Carmel hadn't noticed before.

"I'll walk you out, Carmel," Pam said, gathering her things. "It's a bit of a maze in here."

She waited until the officers had left the room. "Hey kid––you did good. Just one reminder..."

Pam stood close to her and almost whispered. "Don't mention to anybody about you and Darrow," she said. "Like I said, the justice community is too small. Sounds like there are already suspicions about why Darrow didn't haul you up for questioning right away. For his sake, if nothing else, don't breathe a word. He's one of the good guys––we'd hate to lose him."

She was free to go, but what now? The one thing she most wanted to do was run to Darrow and find comfort in his company, but that was verboten. She couldn't put his professional life at risk for her own selfish needs.

Face it, she had nowhere to go except home. Even Sister Constantine, the motherly presence of her child-hood, even she was off on a tour of Rome. And she couldn't go to work for she had no job to go to.

And she simply couldn't face Phonse. Not right now.

She'd never felt lonelier in her life.

Chapter 11

Her car was parked all the way down by the lake, a mile from where she was, and it was raining again, that cold icy rain that is winter's reminder to not get taken in by a sunny March day. The door to the station slammed behind her and she set off across the parking lot.

The Rooms loomed over her. Her natural inclination was to keep going straight and take the short-cut across the front of this building, but she held back for fear of meeting someone she knew. The past hour had shaken her confidence. Laney had made no secret of the fact that he thought she'd killed Marcia, and if he thought that, then a lot of other people probably shared that view. She really just wanted to go hide in a hole somewhere, yes, even with her crippling claustrophobia.

"No," she said aloud, stopping in her tracks. "I can't let that stop me. I'm innocent and I refuse to act like I'm guilty. I'm walking right in front of that place and no one is going to stop me."

As she walked on, she realized that not only was she alone, but she was going to have to prove her own innocence. Laney had made it obvious he wanted to lock her up, and the evidence was not in her favor. Like facts, evidence could be interpreted to the needs of the interpreter. She made up her mind there and then not to crumple, but to be strong and save her own life and freedom if necessary.

So she put head down against the wind and one foot ahead of the other, straight through the puddles and ice and past the parked cars. Just as she drew nigh onto the entrance of the huge building, she heard a tentative voice.

"Carmel?"

A figure in a bright yellow rain coat stood huddled by the corner. It flicked away a cigarette and ran down the wide stairs to meet her. David.

He stopped three feet away from her, gray eyes not flinching in the rain as they stared at her.

"How you doing?" His voice was soft and kind and held no fear that she was a murderer.

"Oh, David," she said. If he was anyone else she would have run for a hug, but David was not a physical kind of person. "Not great. I just came from... there." She indicated the RNC building with her head.

"You didn't get arrested then," he said. There was definitely relief in his voice.

"No, but they want to pin it on me," she said. "David, can we talk?" She hated to ask it of him, but she needed someone on her side.

His eyes glanced left and right, but there was no one around. Inside the glass building, however, there could be any number of watchful eyes.

"Meet me inside the Basilica in ten minutes," he said, nodding his head across the road. The large stone structure sat solidly at the top of the hill overlooking the old downtown. Without another word, he lightly ran up the granite steps to The Rooms.

Across the road and up more stone steps, this time into the Basilica itself. The Catholics kept their building open all day to welcome parishioners and visitors, and had a formidable group of elderly women volunteers to man the giftshop while they kept their beady eyes on anything that could be stolen. Carmel was familiar with the tiny shop from her days growing up with the nuns. You could buy a lot of things in that store––postcards, rosaries, dish towels and saints for every budget.

While waiting for David, she sat in a pew off the centre aisle away from the shop and the volunteers on duty. She leaned her head back and let her eyes drift over the ceiling. This was exactly how she used to pass the long hours of special saint's days and celebrations when she was a child. Her Easter Sunday memories weren't of chocolate bunnies and skipping ropes, but she would always have a new spring dress and a hat and the vaulted ceiling of this building. It went on forever.

David slipped in next to her, his coat leaving wet drops on the polished wooden pew. She was surprised to see him bow his head as if in silent prayer for a moment. His longish hair parted slightly at the back of his neck, baring the soft white skin at his nape.

When he lifted his head again, his luminous gray eyes were unreadable. "Come out to the front porch," he whispered. She followed him out through the doors into the large porch, and he drew her around a corner behind a large pillar.

"So glad I ran into you," he said in a hushed tone. "How are you keeping up?" There was nothing but concern for her in his voice.

Her eyes filled with tears yet again for the umpteenth time this day as her resolve to be strong teetered in the face of his kindness. "You don't think I did it?" she said. "You don't think I killed Marcia?"

"Oh come on. You barely knew her," he said. "You of all people didn't have a reason to do away with her."

"Thank you. That means the world to me." She wiped her nose with the damp sleeve of her jacket. He took a tiny packet of tissues and pressed them into her hand and shook his head when she went to give them back after extracting two.

"I guess I've lost my job over this?" she asked.

"Do you really want to continue to work there?" he asked, slightly incredulous. "After... oh, you know what I mean."

She did know. The shock of finding Marcia's body and the blood on her hands... well, that had little to do with her job, and she knew the memory would fade eventually if she kept her mind off it. But if she didn't go back to work, she would sit at home for hours at a time dwelling on the horror of the events in the basement archive.

And besides that, if she didn't return to the archives, she would have no chance of finding out for herself who murdered the woman. And if she didn't find out, then there was a strong possibility she might lose her freedom, for Laney didn't seem interested in pushing the case beyond the obvious. Darrow was off the case, and Carmel couldn't expect him to imperil his career on her behalf.

She had to go back, there was no choice in the matter. She didn't share this with David, though. Carmel tried to keep her tone light.

"The money is good," she told him. "But I guess suspicion of murdering the top boss is a reason not to pass my probation."

He gave an unexpected laugh and a sympathetic look as if he knew what this had cost her. "Maybe Marcia would have seen it that way," he said. He looked thoughtful, as if turning something over in his mind. "But she's not here anymore. I'm running the Archives now, so you come on back to work on Monday morning."

"You really mean that?" she asked. The day was getting brighter. "But... won't people be uncomfortable?" Much as she had her own reasons for wanting to return to the archives, she hated being ostracized. "You know what folks are like."

"Don't worry about that," he said with his habitual confidence. "If I say you're innocent, then others will accept my example." He paused a moment. "People can be such sheep." She almost thought she heard a hint of a sneer in his voice, but it might have been her imagination.

"I would love to come back," she said. "Really. It's just...."

"The basement," he agreed. "I promise you, you won't ever, ever need to go down there."

David's eyes were focused solely on her right now, enveloping her and soothing, making her feel as if all would be put to right in her world. She wanted to look into his eyes forever for the depths drew her in, and he could see right into her soul. This was a strange sensation, and wasn't sexual in anyway, for David wasn't a sensual creature like that.

"You're feeling pretty low, aren't you?" he asked. "Why don't we get together this weekend?"

"Really, David?" She could hardly believe her ears. He understood her, understood the bleakness of her life at this moment. He had no way of knowing about Darrow, yet he must sense her loneliness despite her efforts to keep up a brave front. "Sure, I can come into town any time."

"I was thinking I'd come out your way," he said. "I'd love to see Captain Jeremy's home."

"You can come for supper tomorrow night," she said, starting to babble in her enthusiasm. This was something to look forward to. The lonely Darrow-less weekend was looking brighter now she had someone believe in her and actively be her friend. "I'll get a group on the go, then we can go to the church, that's a bar now and..."

He held up his hands. "I'm not so into crowds," he warned with a smile on his face. His long lashes dipped over shy eyes.

Of course, he wasn't. David's gift of charisma must be a burden sometimes, everybody wanting a piece of him. She drew back and reciprocated his smile.

"Okay," she said. "Just me and you. That's more comfortable for you, is it?"

He nodded with a small smile. "Thank you."

"I'll see you at my place tomorrow evening then," Carmel said. "Do you need directions?"

"I thought I recognized your voices!" Tina swooped around the corner of the porch niche, making them jump. "What are you guys doing hiding away here? What's happening at your place tomorrow evening?" She looked expectantly from one to the other. The spotlight on the little niche bounced off her glasses.

"Tina..." Carmel began, searching for a way to backtrack. "Well, we were just... what are you doing here?"

"I'm on my way to mass," she replied. Now that she mentioned it, Carmel realized the porch of the Basilica was suddenly busy with people filing through the large doors. "Are you having a dinner party at your place? Can I come? I'll bring my special coconut cream pie——everybody loves that," Tina chattered on as if unaware of her intrusion.

David stared at the floor, refusing to make eye contact with either of them. Carmel was stuck. Common etiquette demanded that Tina be included, for the three worked together after all and Carmel felt she had to extend the invitation to the young woman too.

But she had a niggling suspicion that this meeting in the Basilica was not by chance. Tina could have been watching from across the road in The Rooms and seen David go up the granite steps. It was possible, but how likely was this? And what reasons could she have for following them here? It was with great reluctance that she agreed Tina should join them on Saturday night.

"Why didn't you say something?" Carmel turned on him in frustration after Tina had gone on into the church. The younger woman was beginning to creep her out.

A shrug was his only reply, and his expression was unreadable.

It was only after the heavy door to the Basilica had swung silently after them and they had gone their separate ways that she remembered she'd forgotten to ask him about the map. But there would be lots of time for that this weekend.

Chapter 12

"You can't let your feelings for her cloud your judgement." Evelyn's level voice cut through Darrow's thoughts. She shut the door to his office.

"It's not about my feelings towards her," he insisted. "I know the woman; she's not a murderer." Yes, she had a curious nature, but she was also a lover of art and she was an emotional, sometimes vulnerable, soul. He knew she was innocent, like he knew the spring would come.

Darrow had been sitting at his desk, turned to look out the window at the Southside Hills and feeling very angry. Angry at the unknown circumstances which had led to the murder right next door to the very building he sat in, angry that Inspector Laney was in charge of the case now, but mostly angry at himself for not recognizing sooner the danger he was putting Carmel in through his actions.

"Don't let him lock her up," he said, turning to her. "I'm counting on you, Evelyn."

She gave him a measured look. "You say she didn't do it," Evelyn said, "and I believe you, because it's you saying this. But you know this is not going to be easy."

Evelyn was right, as usual. He knew what they were up against, and he also knew he had mishandled it right from the start––that's what hurt the most. As he had confessed to Hender, the minute he'd seen Carmel, the woman he had almost slept with not twelve hours before that, the moment he heard her name in this case he should have stepped back and allowed another Inspector to take charge. He then would have had a choice of whom to hand the case over to. There were solid inspectors on the Constabulary, educated men and women who didn't have a grudge against Darrow. He could kick himself for being such a selfish bastard and thinking he could protect best Carmel by staying on the case.

"You know there's no secrets in this town," Evelyn reminded him, as if he needed it.

"We went to a movie together and had a coffee afterwards. All in public, nothing to hide."

"You were seen by someone, and now someone has added two and two together to make seven," she continued relentlessly. "And someone told Laney. He'll use this to get back at you if he can."

Of all the officers in the Royal Newfoundland Constabulary who could have been assigned this case, it had to be Inspector Laney. The man was old school, and the two had butted heads even before Darrow had transferred over to the RNC from the national force.

Herb Laney had begun working with the local police as a raw recruit right after ending his career of high school bully. Growing up in the alleys of old downtown

St. John's, he knew every rogue, their grandmother and their priest––he could trace the convoluted relationships of this gene pool throughout the neighborhoods and generations.

This thorough knowledge of the streets made Laney very effective at his job with regards to the small-scale criminals––the druggies, the generational criminals, even the corner boys who had gone on to succeed at politics. His bully's sense of survival was alive and well. Laney knew who he could persecute, and who he had to suck up to, hence his rise through the ranks. Yes, he was effective just as long as his work didn't require subtlety, for those flatfooted boots could never tread lightly. Laney saw only the facts, and his interpretation of them tended to be the quickest route to connect the dots, never minding the picture that lay beneath them waiting to be revealed.

Darrow had lost count of the times that Herb's messes had had to be quietly cleaned up in his wake––the rape victims soothed, the wrongful arrests righted and the questionable level of violence used in arrests covered up by those higher in rank. These incidents took time and public resources to fix, not to mention the toll taken on the victims, yet Laney was in the pockets of the Premier and untouchable under the present government. There was some talk of him moving to head up the Premier's special protection unit. That couldn't come fast enough for Darrow, for surely to God he couldn't do too much damage there.

The thing he feared worst was that the truth of Carmel's innocence could get lost in the picture that Laney's laziness would prefer to draw, that she would be caught in the personal vendetta between the two men.

***

The house was too lonely for her that evening with not even Hank the neighborhood cat to keep her company, so she headed next door to the bar. There was always someone to talk with there.

"Where's your friend Nate tonight?" she asked Bridget.

"Oh, he's off raising funds for the revolution," the red-head said, snickering at the thought.

Phonse took himself away from the pool table as soon as he saw Carmel.

"Any news?"

"They had me in for questioning this morning," she told them. "It's so horrible, being treated like a criminal."

"Darrow did that?" Phonse was scandalized.

"No, some other Inspector," she said. "Darrow can't... he had to hand over the case to that guy. I think he may be in trouble."

"So the man has hung you out to dry?"

"He knows I didn't do it."

"And where does that leave you? Him 'knowing' you didn't commit a murder?" Phonse asked, holding his pool cue in both hands and leaning on it like a staff. "He's not exactly defending you, is he?"

"I think it's complicated," she said, stress showing in her voice. "He had to disclose that we're friends and bow out of the investigation."

"Talk about love 'em and leav 'em. What a scoundrel." Phonse shook his head and signalled to Sid behind the bar. "Don't you think that shows a little bit of disrespect?"

"It's not like that, Phonse," she broke in. Up to this point, Carmel had been worried that Darrow had somehow put his professional career at danger. She hadn't looked at it in this new light that Phonse was presenting.

Had Darrow abandoned her at the first hint of trouble? No, her sensible mind told her, he would never do that. Yet the seed was planted now, and she knew she would worry this like a dog with a rat in its mouth, picking apart the arguments from all directions. Damn Phonse and his suspicious mind.

"Wake up and smell the roses," he said. "What do you think, Sid? This cop dates Carmel. Yeah, we all saw his car at her house that night, and the next day she's up on murder charges and he doesn't lift a finger to help her!"

Sid was silent as he poured up the beers, pondering the issue. He laid the mugs of beer on the counter and thought, one hand smoothing his long luxuriant moustache.

"What can Darrow do about it?" he finally spoke out in his deep voice. "I mean if, as you say, it looks like Carmel is involved, then Darrow can't be on the case. He has to disclose his interest in this."

Phonse rolled his eyes at this. "No gentleman would do that to a lady."

"If it turns out that she's innocent, all well and good, no harm done" said Sid. "On the other hand, if she did murder the woman, then it wouldn't be good practice for Darrow to be investigating, because he would be perceived as looking to prove her innocence, not her guilt."

"Whatever that all means," Phonse said as he screwed up his face. He preferred to see the world in black and white, and philosophical arguments sailed over his head. He turned back to Carmel. "You know you deserve better than this."

Yes, he might be right. For the first time ever, this village idiot might be in the right. Darrow had walked away from her, leaving her to the mercy of that horrible Inspector Laney and the distinct possibility that she would be charged with murder. Darrow was looking after his own professional reputation, and he'd thrown her under the bus to save himself.

Phonse took a long swallow of beer, belched contemplatively, then continued, "You get yourself into the worst kind of situations. And you know what? Have you noticed that I'm the one who always has to pick up the pieces when things happen to you? I have to drive you to the hospital every time you fall off a rock or trip in a pothole or get locked up by a crazy woman. And now I'm the only one talking sense to you about a guy who's dropped you like a hot potato at the first sign of trouble."

Carmel hunched down on her bar stool, feeling low. She'd thought she'd been pretty okay till Phonse had started his rant.

"Oh," he said, seeing her deflation. He placed a heavy arm around her and bending down to her. "I didn't mean to upset you. It just... it bugs me when I see someone hurting you like this. You know I care."

She leaned into his hold. It was small comfort, but right now she would take comfort from wherever it was offered. Carmel felt tears not too far away yet again.

"You know, my offer still stands," he whispered in her ear. "We can get married, and you won't have to worry about jerks like Darrow ever again."

That hit her like a splash of cold water on a winter night, waking her out of her self-pity party. Carmel sat up and pushed his arm away. "No, we can't marry, Phonse. There's nothing between us and it would just be wrong. And I don't want Vee as a mother-in-law!"

He took rejection well, only shrugging as he returned to his beer. "You're missing your chance," he told her. "You know I'm going to be rich, don't you?"

"And how are you ever going to make money, Phonse? What, you're going to get a job?" The man had never held a job in his life. For tax purposes and on paper, Phonse was a fisherman, but she never saw him unloading fish from his wharf and he only ever took the boat out at night. Each day after one of his trips, the bikers in the bar would be transporting mysterious cargo from the church. Best not to think too hard on that one.

"A job? Don't be so foolish," he said. "No, Cap'n Jem's treasure is going to make me rich. Did you get hold of the map yet?"

"How am I going to get my hands on the map? It's probably being used as evidence. Although," she brightened, "I didn't lose my job after all. David wants me to come back on Monday. Even with the potential charges hanging over my head."

"There you go," Phonse said. "I knew you'd come through for me."

She was thoughtful for a moment. David was interested in maps, perhaps he would help her with this. And she wouldn't steal the map––no, a photocopy of it would be fine. She could do this.

"Remember, I'm counting on you as a friend," Phonse pressed before she left the bar that night. "We really need that map".

Chapter 13

T he fifteen-year-old girl flicked her hair in annoyance. "Well, the woman you were out with the other night is a murderer, so I don't think you're a very good judge of who I can hang out with." Dani threw her words like knives. "That's what Bradley said. His dad told him so."

Do not react, Darrow told himself. It was hard sometimes. Most times. She was her mother's daughter, and it wasn't her fault.

"Bradley Dickson's dad has no business discussing police work with his son," he told her, giving up all hope of a quiet Saturday night in front of the fireplace with a single malt, a good book and his dog. It was almost enough to make him lift Dani's latest grounding and send her out into the world to look for more trouble, just to give him the selfish peace he craved. "And why is Constable Dickson talking about my personal life?"

He looked at his daughter over his reading glasses, fixing her with what he hoped was a stern glare.

She heaved a sigh and plopped herself down on the faded beige sofa, losing herself in her phone, the better to ignore him. No, there would be little peace for him tonight.

"Irn needs a walk," he told her. At this, the rust-colored Newfoundland dog at his side sat up pretty quick for an old guy.

"I'm grounded," she said as her thumbs quickly worked her phone.

"Dog walking in the park doesn't count. That's a duty, not a social occasion." Having the large expanse of Bannerman Park behind their Monkstown Road townhouse had more than made up for the lack of backyard space over the years. The kids had grown up with the city's swimming pool, swings and acreage as their personal playground, and the bonus was that he was not required to do any maintenance on the extensive grounds.

Irn woofed to voice his opinion on the matter.

"Fine," she said, huffing. So much of her vocabulary these days consisted of expressive outlets of air. She sent a final text and got to her feet.

"And I'll be watching you from the stair landing," he reminded her, for she had given in too soon––this had been too easy. She was up to something. "Don't stray."

"Why don't you just put a chip in my neck to track my movements?"

"I don't need to––I've got the GPS activated on your phone and connected to the computer system at work. I dare you to leave it behind." He rarely lied to his children, but this was an effective threat as it was a possibility. Of course, this technology was beyond him, and he would never ask his more technically savvy subordinates to spend police resources on his personal life, but Dani couldn't be sure of that.

The strength of the door slamming on her way out rocked through the three-story wooden house. Darrow's eye was caught by an old photo on the mantel piece, a snapshot of happier days when the kids and dog were young.

The Newfoundland, still a pup, was standing in the sunlight with Dani and Angus sprawled around him with the green of the Park's expansive lawns as their backdrop. They were five and two-years-old respectively. The dog's coat, caught by the sun and fluffed by the wind, looked like an orange sunburst all around him.

"He's the color of Irn Bru," Fiona had cried with delight when she first saw the round little puppy. The other national drink of Scotland was an unnaturally orange fizzy drink loaded with sugar and caffeine, and the name had stuck, for Irn had the energy to match. Newfoundland dogs were normally black or white, the only colors acceptable to the dog breeders and competitors, so Irn's rusty coloring had disbarred him from the competitions. This had made him affordable to a policeman with a growing family and an artistic wife who refused to work or use her own money for her upkeep.

Looking back on his relationship with Fiona, he could now see that the dog, even the children and their marriage, had all been part of her attempts to achieve happiness and self-fulfilment, a goal which she had never reached while living in Canada. Not long after adopting the young puppy, the winds of her whims had blown her back to her native Scotland, back to her father's estate and his money and the aristocratic set she'd grown up with. Fiona had tired of slumming it.

If she hadn't come from a moneyed background, she might have been diagnosed as mentally ill somewhere along the line and been given the real help she needed. As it was, she could afford to be eccentric and live her erratic unhappy life to its fullest.

Those early years had been rough, but the family had found a saviour in Mrs. O'Keefe. A widowed nurse who'd taken early retirement when her own family was grown, she'd descended on his household like a modern-day Mary Poppins, delighted to be needed and to have a project. Mrs. O's official title was 'housekeeper,' but Darrow preferred to call her his 'home-keeper.' She chose her hours according to the needs of the children and Darrow's work and provided a stable base for all while living in the connected apartment on the back of the house. Her salary was paid by Fiona's father with no quibbles from that landed gentleman.

The front door to the townhouse opened, then a cautious knock sounded.

"You home?" Evelyn Wright's voice called out.

"In here," Darrow raised his voice to reply.

She hesitated at the living room doorway after leaving her boots in the porch. "I saw you through the window," she said. "If this isn't convenient I can leave again."

"Come in and sit a while. Drink?"

"Rum and coke if you have it," she replied. "Don't get up; I'll help myself."

He threw another birch log on the fire and stirred up the embers while he waited. She took the seat on the sofa vacated by Danielle.

"You should really lock your front door," she noted. Evelyn's shoulder-length blond hair was loose tonight, brushed straight and gleaming. It always took him aback to see her hair down. Secretly, he preferred it up, for the heavy curtain overwhelmed the fine bone structure of her face. The workaday ballet dancer's bun suited her much better.

"Kids," he said, and she nodded in understanding.

"And you should surely be home with your family on a Saturday night," he said. "I know you've come to discuss work."

She laughed. "You caught me," she replied. "I'd rather be here. My mother-in-law is visiting and I just can't handle it."

"Mmmn," said Darrow, not committing his opinion either way. "And Bruce?"

Evelyn leaned back into the comfortable sofa with her drink in her hand, unmindful of the dog and cat fur. "Oh, you know he's out at the Police Club with the guys," she said, then sighed. "It's gotten worse since my promotion."

"I can only imagine."

No one would deny that Evelyn and Bruce had a rocky relationship. He'd been willing enough to accept her as an equal partner financially, meaning she kept working after the twins were born even though she was expected to take care of all the child-rearing and housework, but now that Evelyn outranked him, her life was no doubt getting rough. Add to the mix her hag of a mother-in-law who thought the sun shone out of her son's nether regions and that Evelyn was a lazy, neglectful spouse, well... He didn't envy her.

Evelyn Wright was the strongest woman he knew, and he had no doubt she would one day outstrip even his own rank, if only she wasn't hampered by that brute of a husband.

"I've had a disturbing report from Dani," he said. "You know she's friendly with Dickson's son?"

Evelyn shook her head in disgust. "Don't tell me," she said. "He's spreading tales outside work."

"That's one constable who'll be put on traffic duty for the next year," he noted. He let a pause fall in the conversation, to give his sergeant room to bring up what they both needed to discuss.

"There's been no movement on the case," she finally said. "We've got no fingerprints or hairs on the body, no identifiable motives, nothing. The cover-all they found in the toilet had nothing inside it. Some hairs were stuck to the outside, but those wouldn't stand up in court. It could be argued they were previously on the floor where it was thrown. And yes, before you ask——one of them could match up with McAlistair's. But the testing won't be back for weeks yet."

"And the cameras were not hooked up," Darrow said. "Cost saving measure compliments of the provincial government. So it can't be proved who was in the vicinity, even to rule them out of the genetic matching."

"It's a puzzle. No one has access behind the scenes, nobody else was in the basement, everyone's movements were accounted for in as much as they can be," she said. "Except for..."

He nodded. "Except for Ms. McAlistair."

"Tina White, the desk clerk, has given an account of everybody who passed through into the back. She claims she was either at the desk or just inside the back rooms during the time frame."

Darrow picked up on Evelyn's emphasis. "Claims? You have reason to doubt her?"

A log on the fire sparked and crackled, flaring up. She watched it burn out behind the fire screen. "Not that I doubt her," she said, choosing her words with care. "It's just... oh, that girl's had such a hard life, and I never had the feeling that she's quite all there. Her mom is Dorrie."

"Dorrie of the courthouse?" Darrow was referring to a well-known prostitute and drug addict who had staked out her claim years ago on the Duckworth Street entrance of the courthouse as her 'turf,' after normal business hours, of course. Dorrie was, quite simply, a wreck, and it never ceased to amaze him how the woman's body still functioned after all those years of self-abuse.

Evelyn nodded. "Exactly," she said. "Tina grew up down the road from me. Mom used to try to help the girl anyway she could. And you know, Dorrie used to be an upstanding citizen once upon a time. She worked as a secretary in the Clerkwell law offices downtown. I remember seeing her go off to work every day, done up like a stick of gum, not a hair out of place. But she fell pregnant, her parents threw her out of the house, and it was all downhill from there. Dorrie's still very bitter against lawyers in general. Probably why she chooses to sell her wares on the courthouse steps."

"You don't feel Tina's a reliable witness," he said.

Evelyn shook her head. "She's an odd one. I never get the feeling she's telling the whole truth, that she's always hiding something."

Darrow thought another moment. "Are all the witnesses sure about Dr. Taverstock?"

Evelyn shrugged. "You know how it is," she said. "Everyone saw him go through to the back, but no one was keeping a close eye on the clock. He could have nipped down to the basement and been back upstairs within the time limit, but I really don't see him moving that fast."

"But he could have, if he had reason to do it," he said. "And Tina said he left in a tearing hurry without saying good-bye, which admittedly was not unusual for him."

"He's not ruled out, but Laney isn't pushing that side of the investigation."

"David Clerkwell?"

"Again, he was seen going into his own office," replied Evelyn. "But then the departmental secretary went out on lunch break and when she returned, he was in the bathroom throwing up after finding the body."

"The use of the doorstop to kill her points to this being a spur of the moment murder," Darrow said reflectively.

"But what could be the motive?" Evelyn asked. "Marcia Flynn, not well-liked it seems, but no reason to kill her."

"She hadn't had a fight with anyone? Nothing coming out like that?"

The woman shook her head no. "The usual quibbles you'll find in any environment with intelligent people stuck in an office together for years, I guess more so given her personality, but no one is speaking too ill of the dead."

"Not your impression that anyone was hiding something?"

"No, they were all straight forward enough to admit she was bossy, rude and abrupt. They all hated her, but I think they were used to her ways."

"And the alarm which was set off at the fire door––any sightings of the killer hopping over the gate on Harvey Road?"

"None. There were plenty of people who came forward to say they drove by at about that time, but no-one saw anything odd."

They both became lost in thought as they sipped their drinks by the fire.

"Could it have been a cover-up for a theft?" Darrow wondered out loud. "How valuable are the papers and books kept down there?"

"According to David, some things are very valuable, and others are priceless but only because they have historical value," Evelyn said. "Not something you could sell on the black market, not even like stolen artwork.

Who would want to buy, say, the receipt for fish sales from 1621? It's just not sexy at all."

"He's done an inventory?"

"David checked the valuable papers and books for us, but not a thorough inventory of the basement and archives, no," she added, "I did advise Laney this needs to be done. It would be a huge undertaking, and I'm not sure the resources are in place for that."

"Laney!" Darrow spit. "I'm guessing he still wants to pin it on Carmel?"

Evelyn gave him a level glance. "Well, she was found on the scene with the victim's blood all over her hands. Nobody else was even in the vicinity."

"It's ridiculous. She would have had to thump the woman on the head, open the fire door out by the stairs, thrown the cover-all in the washroom, all in some order, and then run back and stuck her hands in the blood and then wait to be found? And it was in the dark, she could never have voluntarily shut herself in the dark. It doesn't make sense."

"Perhaps Laney's not looking at the finer points of making sense," Evelyn noted.

"But what motive does he think the woman had to kill someone she barely knows?"

"He mentioned professional jealousy."

"What bloody nonsense! She's not an archivist. She only has a bachelor's degree, and was delighted to have the position of Assistant to the Assistant."

"Something else we don't know about? Perhaps they had a secret quarrel that no one else witnessed. You didn't pick up anything from her did you?"

Darrow knew she was only throwing out suggestions into the creative space he had always encouraged amongst his team, but it took a lot for him not to deny them as accusations. "There's no earthly reason that Carmel would murder Flynn," he said flatly.

Evelyn sighed.

"What?" Darrow turned to look at his sergeant.

"There's the fact that she lives in St. Jude Without," she said. "That in itself raises flags for most of the RNC. And the RCMP, for that matter."

"She's not from there, and isn't related to anyone from the place." He scowled, his heavy brows almost meeting at the center, then threw back the rest of his drink. "Another one?" he asked, indicating his empty glass as he stood up.

Evelyn shook her head. "I'm driving." She watched him pour the Scotch from the bottle on the side table, then continued to press her point. "Nothing good comes from that place, as you well know."

"It wasn't her!" he found himself almost shouting at Evelyn. He stopped and stared at her, aghast at his action.

There was a long pause.

"And that's why you should have taken yourself off the case the minute we saw her in the basement," she said.

He nodded, silent now and not a little embarrassed.

"Look," she said, in a far kinder tone, "McAlistair is the only one who had the chance to do this. That we know of, anyway. I don't know what her motive could have been, but we all know that Laney doesn't worry himself too much about niceties like that."

He shook his head yet again, slowly this time. "It's almost as if she was being set up," he said, his voice thoughtful.

There was no reply to this one. Darrow glanced over to Evelyn. She didn't meet his eye, but stood up with her glass and made her way to the kitchen where he could hear the sounds of another drink being poured.

When she'd returned to her seat, Evelyn took a long sip then leaned forward on the old sofa. "Set up? Are you serious about that?"

"It's an avenue to explore," Darrow replied. "Hypothetically. Haven't I always taught you to search out every explanation?"

"And who is Carmel McAlistair that someone would be out to get her?" she asked. "What is her importance? Hypothetically, of course."

Darrow caught the pity in her eye before a mask came down and shut her emotions out. It was hard to stomach for he wasn't used to seeing doubt expressed toward him from his sergeant. Before he could say anything, she jumped back in as if to a chore which had to be gotten out of the way.

"She's important to you," Evelyn admitted, nodding her head. "But seriously? With all due respect, I can't see that this case, this murder, has anything to do with her."

"But why was Marcia murdered when Carmel was in the very room?" he asked. "If someone wanted to kill the woman, why not do it when there would be no potential witnesses?"

"Why does that woman always find bodies––what is it with her?" Evelyn asked in return.

Darrow was still thinking hard and ignored the observation. "She is important to me, and it appears to be no secret."

His sergeant cocked her head, seeing where he was going. "Someone trying to get at you?" There was doubt in her voice.

"Is this just paranoid thinking?"

"Might be," Evelyn admitted. "On the other hand, maybe not. But why?"

"I've made a few enemies over the years..."

"That's true," she said. "But not in the archive division. Unless you've been up to something on the side I don't know about?" This last was accompanied by a smile. "Defacing old books perhaps?"

He laughed with her, the tension broken, and placed his hand down by the side of the chair to ruffle the old dog's fur, but his hand met empty air. "Christ, Dani and the dog aren't back yet!"

"She's taking the dog for a walk on a Saturday night?" Evelyn said. "Looks like somebody's grounded."

He was on the phone to his daughter right away. "No, you're correct, I didn't specify how long you could be. What are you doing out there?"

Darrow listened, shaking his head at Evelyn.

"All your friends just happened to be out at the Loop on a week-end night," he repeated. "And you're just having a Beaver Tail." This delicacy was a new treat to brighten up the St. John's winter––deep fried pastry with an assortment of toppings available. The perfect thing for the after-skate at the rink in the park; melted chocolate somehow tasted better when one's cheeks were red with cold.

"Well, finish it, and come right back," he told her, playing the stern dad. "I'm watching for you on the landing. Don't dawdle."

Evelyn stood up to leave. "Much as I'd love to, I can't stay to watch the fireworks," she joked. "Thank God I've got boys and don't have this to look forward to." Her five-year-old twins were right little terrors, but when they grew older, teen-age boys didn't cause their parents to have the same horrors that girls did, for the boys were allowed the freedom to get into trouble.

After seeing her out, Darrow stayed by the door, sunk in thought. If someone was out to get back at Carmel or perhaps himself, who would it be? There was only one answer to that question.

Ruscan Milanovic, her ex-lover. The man who had followed her here to Newfoundland and refused to leave. All of Darrow's information said the Ukranian was a sketchy customer with criminal ties to gangs all over Asia and Russia.

He was at a loss to see how Ruscan could have engineered the murder, but felt sure a man of his criminal tendencies could manage to sidestep the security system of an institution which didn't even bother putting the CC cameras into action. Why Ruscan would do this was another matter and the only answer Darrow could find was jealousy––was it a coincidence the murder had happened after they'd started seeing each other?

What a ridiculous idea. Still, perhaps it was time to pay a visit to the rusted hulk in the harbor that Ruscan called home.

He couldn't bear to do nothing to help Carmel.

Chapter 14

M eanwhile in St. Jude Without that same Saturday night, Carmel welcomed David and Tina into her home. They had arrived in separate cars. Tina started chattering the moment she arrived, not noticing David's silence.

"No problem finding the place, then?" Carmel broke in as she shut out the March wind and offered them a choice of thick hand-made wool socks left by the previous owners in the carton by the door. Even with the heating on, the draughts of the ancient house required cozy layers to be worn.

"I love this old house," Tina said loudly as she handed Carmel the pie. "It's so quaint."

David winced, just a little. This was going to be a difficult evening trying to negotiate between the two. It could have been avoided if David had spoken up in the Basilica, found a story to put Tina off.

He finally spoke when he entered the kitchen. "How absolutely retro!" he exclaimed, looking all around him.

"Retro," Carmel repeated, eyeing her kitchen which hadn't seen changes for decades. She'd put in a stacked washer dryer (so she didn't have to do laundry in the cellar), but other than that, the kitchen remained as she had bought it with its mis-hung turquoise cupboard doors, wheezy fridge and paint-thickened ancient wooden chairs. "Yeah, you like what I've done with it?"

"Authentic Bay, circa 1970," he said, and laughed. "Seriously, it's cozy. Don't change a thing."

Tina's expression didn't convey the same delight in her surroundings, but now she was ensconced in the house, at least her chattering had stopped.

Carmel indicated for them to take seats at the table. "I've made Irish stew," she said. "My tenant showed me how to make the real thing. He's Irish."

"Tenant?" David asked. "Is he joining us?"

She shook her head. "No, Ian's out touring with his band. He doesn't actually spend a lot of time here, as his girlfriend Bridget lives across the road. The rent helps with the bills though."

"So just us tonight?" He cast a glance at Tina.

"Guess so, unless we get visitors," she said. "You know what it's like in a small place; they're probably all wondering who owns the strange cars in my driveway, and they may send up a delegation to check you out."

"Oh," he said.

He's not into crowds, she remembered, and turned away from the oven where she'd lifted out the stew pot. It was probably hard enough for him with Tina here. She got the sense from him that the young woman's presence got on his nerves, and adding more people into the mix would be way too difficult for him to handle. "I can discourage people from visiting," she told him. Wiping her hands, she nipped out to the front door and pulled down the blind to send the 'unwelcome' signal to any curious nosy parkers.

Her reputation was going to be in tatters––the second male visitor in less than a week. Worse than last summer when the whole cove watched her go out to Bell Island with Phonse in his little boat, Carmel totally unaware that such a trip signified they had sexual intentions, but Phonse proudly showing off to all and sundry. Of course they didn't do anything, but that didn't stop the gossip. Especially from Phonse's mother Vee Ryan, who kept a special hole for Carmel in her shrivelled hate-filled heart.

"Okay, hopefully I've stopped the crowds from descending upon us," she laughed as she dished out the stew and explained about the code. "Everyone understands about the need for privacy in such a closed-in community. They don't like it, but they'll respect it."

David relaxed a little and smiled as he accepted his plate. "And it will give their tongues something to wag about."

Tina still stayed silent, her eyes going back and forth between the two. Her silence was beginning to be a little unnerving.

After a moment, though, David put down his spoon and turned to Carmel. "I have to ask, because I've been so worried about you," he began. "You may not even want to talk about it. But that was a horrible thing you went through. How are you really doing?"

Carmel felt the back of her eyes sting as tears threat-
ened at his kindness, yet again. She blinked them back
and took a deep breath. "You're right; it was awful," she
said. "The dark, and then Marcia...But I've survived it. I
just try not to think about it."

He nodded.

"You also got a shock," she reminded him.

"I'm sorry," he said. "So sorry for leaving you there. I
wasn't thinking when I saw you. It was just so unspeak-
ably grim." He was silent for a moment. "I actually ran
away from it all. I ran and ran up the stairs until I found
the bathroom, and I started throwing up."

She almost smiled at the thought of David, so neat and
prim and proper, actually throwing up in public.

"What happened, anyway?"

Carmel took a deep breath and began to re-tell the
story.

"I thought she called out to me, so I called back," she
said. "Then I heard her scream and the lights went out.
I don't know how long it took me to make my way back
up through the stacks in the dark––it felt like an hour,
but was probably just a few minutes. And then––well,
you know."

"I couldn't figure out what had happened to you," he
said. "I'd asked you to hurry––and sorry about that, I
know I get involved in something and lose patience with
people. But you'd disappeared, and Marcia was nowhere
to be found either. When I came down the back stairs,
I could hear the alarm going off––I assumed it was just

someone slipped out for a moment, you know how they do."

"I never did get those files I asked you to get for me," Tina finally broke in, her voice plaintive. The other two paused in their flow to glance at her, then carried on.

"The alarm!" Carmel said. "I'd forgotten about that. I thought at the time it was just my head pounding, but I guess it was the door alarm going off. It was muffled through the closed door to the archives, it sounded so far away." She thought about it for a moment more. "Why didn't you turn the alarm off when you were passing, if you were on the stairs?"

He looked at her with surprise. "I guess... I assumed the person who'd opened it would be coming back in. I didn't want to lock them out. And besides," he went on, "I was really worried about you, because I know you hate the basement. When I turned the corner and saw the door closed, I thought... I didn't know what to think."

"And then you opened the door..."

"Yes, and had to switch on the light. And there you were..."

They were both silent for another moment before they picked up their spoons again.

"You know," David began, then looked at her quickly. "Not to harp on this, but the police had very specific questions about Tony Taverstock."

He paused, then continued, "Maybe I shouldn't be telling you this, but... Oh well. I had to tell them about all the fights between Marcia and him over the years, and that a certain Squires' folder is missing."

Her lack of comprehension must have been evident, so he filled her in. Sir Richard Squires had been premier of the country of Newfoundland, way back before Confederation and even the Second World War, and was Tony's particular niche of study. The original disagreement between the two had stemmed from Marcia not allowing Tony's library to hold that very set of documents, even though he had been the one to unearth them in a second hand junk shop. The two had been sworn enemies since that time.

"Tony's not a very nice man," Tina finally spoke up. "He's always so rude to me, like I'm beneath him or something. I could see him as the murderer, no problem."

That man with the braces and pot belly a killer? Carmel had a hard time picturing it. "Didn't you say you saw him leaving?"

"He was in a big rush," Tina replied, her eyes sliding off to the side. "He already had his coat on. He might have been hiding something."

"Like... bloodstains?"

Tina considered. "I wouldn't put it past him," she said. "He hated Marcia so much."

"More likely he was stealing the Squires folder," David said in a low voice.

As they continued to eat, Carmel searched for a way to bring up the old map from the chest. She truly doubted it was the treasure map Phonse claimed it to be—that was the stuff of children's fiction, just the sort of thing to appeal to the man-child he was.

The question was, how to bring it up to David without appearing to be an idiot, a member of the Facebook tribe who thrived on half facts and fantasies. Unfortunately, Carmel had never learned to be subtle when it was most required, so she brought it up plain and simple. She really should have prepared a plan.

"The map from the chest," she said, "the one that Marcia had..."

David paused, spoon half way to his mouth.

"Do you suppose I could get a closer look at it?"

He flashed her a glance from beneath his curtain of hair. "Why?" He set himself back to eating. Ian's stew recipe really was delicious.

She shrugged, and ate a mouthful herself to give her time to think. Tina was back to watching the two closely.

"Well," she said, swallowing, "I find it sort of interesting. I mean, someone went to the trouble of creating the map in the first place, so it must have had a purpose. It would be interesting to see if we recognize what it's a map of."

"We?"

"Uh, you and me?"

"I'm sure it's nothing. Garbage really, just like the old clothes it was found with."

"Mmmn," she said and continued to push. "No doubt. But Darrow said it was a map of St. Jude Without, and I'm curious."

"Your boyfriend? The man I met the other night. Isn't he a police officer?"

"You're going out with a cop?" Tina interjected.

"Not my boyfriend," she said quickly. "Just a friend."

"When did he see the map?" David asked.

"The RNC were called down to the Clerkwell premises when they found the skeleton and the chest together," she reminded him. "Darrow was there."

"Oh," David said. "I had no idea."

"He said there was not much marked on it, that it was really just half a map," Carmel said. "Still, I wouldn't mind having a look at it, too. Just, you know, for the sake of interest."

"Half a map," David said, slowly. "Of course."

"So, can I have a look at it?"

"Oh, I have no idea where it got to," David said, dismissing the map now. "Marcia had it, and she wasn't sharing."

"Yes, I saw it in the basement with her, but she grabbed it and wouldn't let me see it," Carmel said. "And then... well."

"I guess it's probably been taken up as evidence then," David said, losing interest in the topic. "Ask your boyfriend, he'll be able to show it to you."

"He's not..."

"I saw the map," Tina cut in as if tired of being left out of the conversation. "If it's just half a map, where would the rest of it be?"

"I really don't think it's that important," David said, addressing Tina for perhaps the first time that evening. "Why would anyone care about a half a map?"

"If the map is of this cove," Tina persisted. "Do you think it's from the pirate Jeremy Ryan?"

The other two stopped and stared at her.

"How do you know about Captain Jem?" Carmel asked, the wonder evident in her voice. David said nothing.

"I've read all the diaries, you know," Tina replied, nodding her head at David. "All those ones you donated to the archives after writing your Master's thesis. I'm not just another pretty face."

"Oh," said Carmel, "so I guess you know of the link between the Clerkwells and the Ryans."

"I probably know more about the Clerkwell family than you do, David," Tina said archly. She leaned closer over the table, her eyes on him. "I find them very fascinating. And I think that map, the map that Marcia had——I think it might be a treasure map!" She gazed at the other two to judge their reaction to her news.

This was not good. The girl was a chatterer. If she suspected the map might lead to Captain Jem's treasure, the news might quickly spread all through the city. She'd have it on Facebook in no time. A vision of St. Jude Without overrun by treasure seekers, armed with spades and compasses, flashed before Carmel's eyes. Phonse would be severely pissed if that happened, and she knew he would find a way to blame her.

David's face was a blank. He drew a breath as if to speak, but Carmel got there first. She had to stop the treasure-tourists before they began to swarm the cove.

"That's cracked," she blurted out. "I mean, what treasure? There may be old stories, but come on, do you really put any substance in those? That's like... I mean, look around you at this cove. Do you really think there's anywhere to bury treasure? Where? There's no topsoil around here, just rocks."

"There's a farm up the road," Tina said in a truculent voice. She was reluctant to give up on her brilliant idea. "It might be buried there."

"Clyde only grows potatoes," Carmel quickly said. "It's really rocky soil."

"Isn't there a graveyard out back? If they could bury bodies, they could bury treasure," Tina shot back triumphantly.

Carmel was astounded by how much Tina knew about the cove. You'd think she had a personal connection or something, yet she'd never seen the young woman around here before.

"Treasure?" she repeated with a small laugh. "I'm sure there's no treasure out there. Just dead Ryans." She shook her head for emphasis.

"I doubt if any treasure would have survived in this cove for long," David said as he finally spoke up. "But I bet there's all sorts of interesting things in this house, though."

Carmel welcomed the change of subject, but she had to be honest with him. "The Ryans were packrats, but they only seemed to have saved junk," she said.

"Captain Jeremy's original house and no––say––bits of old paper left around? Nothing in the bookshelves?"

The cover of the red Pirates of Newfoundlande book flashed to her mind, the one that seemed to jump from its home in the bookcase at odd times. David was interested in Captain Jem, and surely it would steer the conversation away from buried treasures.

"Yes," she said, jumping up from the table. "I have a book you might like to see. Let me go get it."

She searched the floor to ceiling book case in the living room, but darned if she could find it. There was the space it lived in, that she had firmly shoved it into the other night, but no pirate book.

The book in question was one of many left by the previous owner of the house who had fled the cove a week after his wife passed on. "That's weird," she said aloud. Perhaps Phonse had borrowed it without telling her, to further his research into the supposed trove of treasure hiding in the cove. Best hold her tongue.

"What is?" David's voice loomed over her shoulder, making her jump.

"Oh, a book that was here," she said, shifting the books on either side of the space to cover up the hole.

"Where did it go?"

"Someone took a loan of it, probably," she assured him. "I'll show it to you another time."

He cast a dismissive glance over the remaining books on the shelves. "Nothing too exciting here, by the looks of it," he said. "Mostly westerns from the last century."

He drummed his fingers on the back of the old red sofa. "There has to be interesting things in this house somewhere," he said.

"There's just a lot of junk, really," Carmel said. "The Ryans just kept all the broken stuff that might come in handy someday, but really should all have gone to the dump or burned."

She told him about the old dresser Ian had found in the cellar, the one with two of three drawers working. If it hadn't been so scuffed up and ill-worn, it might have been worth something to those who liked ancient home-made furniture.

His eyes were alight again. "The cellar! You must take me down there."

Chapter 15

"Not the cellar," Carmel found herself saying in shock. Was he mad? After the experience of finding Marcia's dead body in the last dark basement she'd been in, this was the last place she wanted to go. "You're not getting me down there!"

There was kindness deep within his eyes as he looked at her with understanding. "It's okay," he said and when he said that, she could almost believe it was true. "I understand about the phobia. But Carmel, you need to confront this while it's still fresh. Get back on the horse. I'm going to be with you, and this is your chance to work through it."

The five-year-old in her was screaming '*no, no, not so soon after Marcia's murder*,' and the warm sticky blood on her hands, but he was mesmerizing her again with his eyes.

"You really should have been offered professional help right at the time, you know. You could develop PTSD from that experience. The police were lax in their duty," he told her. "I'm not a counsellor, but I do understand things like this. Going down into that cellar right now will help you in the long run, and I'll hold your hand the whole time," he continued, laying his hand on her shoulder. It was a cool touch through her sweater. Seeing her waver, he nodded with encouragement. "You can do it."

"There's no lights down there. We won't be able to see a thing."

"You have a flashlight?"

She nodded with reluctance, seeing her arguments slipping away.

"Okay then, we have light. I'll be with you the whole time," he said again. "You need to do this, and you're strong."

The old cellar door creaked as he pushed it open to show the old wooden steps that led down into the dark.

"I'm not going down there," Tina declared as she peered through the open doorway. "It's disgusting."

"Suit yourself," David said, almost under his breath.

Carmel prayed that Phonse would find out the lengths she was going to to save his stupid pirate treasure which was probably nonexistent anyway. "No darbies down there?" She tried to make light of it, although her heart was pounding.

"I can guarantee it's darby free," David said solemnly. "Whatever they are, they're certainly not down here."

"They're the dark creatures," she said, putting off the moment of descent. "They eat kids."

"Well, I guess we're safe then," he said with a little laugh as he took her hand. "We're all grown-up, and they don't exist anyway."

They both removed their woolly socks and put on their footgear. He went down first, shining the flashlight on the rickety steps while still holding her hand tight. There was no bannister to cling to, so they both huddled to the damp stone wall of the foundation.

"Smells bad down here," she said, holding back. It wasn't a sour smell, just musty and rotting and hinting of dead creatures.

"It's a disused cellar," he told her, being the voice of reason. "It probably floods every spring with the runoff from the mountain."

David shone the flashlight onto the ground when they reached the bottom. Standing on the dirt floor, Carmel sighed with relief and loosened her hold on David's shoulder. She didn't even realize she'd been gripping him so tightly.

The dirt of the floor was dry, as it was still March and the snow hadn't melted off the hills behind the cove yet. It was cool down here but not freezing like it was outside. David shone the flashlight around the surprisingly large space.

Brick pillars held up the weight of the house in arches that seemed to stretch on forever, while the foundation walls were made of granite boulders, smaller cousins to the giants which littered the roadside to St. Jude Without. In the wavering light, their rounded sides were spotted with moss and lichen, looking organic as if the walls themselves were alive and breathing. Shadows jumped out all around as David flashed the light back and forth in the cellar.

Rough wooden walls had been thrown up as divisions in some parts, the salt-scarred timber looking as if it had been scrounged from shipwrecks washed up in the cove from centuries before. Odd shapes of discarded furniture and implements jumped out of the shadows as he flashed the light around.

"See? It's not so bad down here. It's just an empty space."

David casually lifted the lid of a rough wooden box close at hand; it looked like a huge vegetable bin. He let the heavy top drop when he saw there was nothing inside. The next item at hand was a dusty barrel, but that too held little interest for him.

Before she knew it, David was hurriedly searching through the most promising bits of old furniture and wooden cartons, lifting rotten canvases and old fishing nets and creating a fog of dust in the beam of the single light. He brought his sweater over his face as a mask, becoming himself an unrecognizable shape in the shifting light.

"David?" Carmel hated the quaver she heard in her voice, echoing through the brick arches. He'd left her behind, no longer holding her hand as he'd promised, and he was already halfway across the cavernous space.

"Oh right," he said in an impatient tone and shone the beam directly at her eyes. Now she could see nothing at all. "Well, keep up with me." He went back to his search.

Still blinded by the afterimage on her retina, she reached out in his direction but stumbled over a large wooden object that leapt into her path. Her foot hooked into something and she went down on one knee with a crash.

"Ow!!" She struggled to free herself but was caught in a web of hard edges and pain. There was blood somewhere; she just didn't know where it was coming from.

"For God's sake!" he exclaimed and hurried over to help disentangle her from the wooden cart wheel that was crucifying her. It had been leaning up against some cracked wooden kitchen chairs, the reed seats long ago worn thin by Ryan bottoms.

They could hear Tina squawking from the top of the stairs, demanding to know what had happened.

"I'm bleeding," Carmel cried with tears of fright running down her cheeks. Panic was engulfing her mind, and the need for flight quickly overtook her. Carmel pushed David aside and aimed for the light at the top of the cellar steps. "I've to get out of here!"

"Careful on those stairs," he called to her, then gave a last flick around with the flashlight. "I don't think there's much down here anyway. No papers could have survived the damp."

She half scrabbled, half climbed up to the light on her hands and knees, driven by the panic that had been unleashed, that which had lurked at the back of her mind since she was a child. Once safely in the light of the kitchen, she wanted nothing more than to shut the cellar door and crawl under the table.

The apology in David's eyes was evident as he bent down to peer at her. He extended his hand. "Oh,

Carmel," he said, "I'm so sorry. Come on out from under there."

They were both filthy in the warm light of the kitchen. David's crisp jeans were smeared with dust and there were cobwebs in his hair. Tina stared open-mouthed at the pair.

"You've cut your knee," he said to Carmel with concern. "Those pants are ruined now. Run up and change, and I'll wash your wounds. Do you have any antibiotic cream?"

"Not likely," she said, sniffing back the last of the tears. "Try the little cupboard over by the sink."

Carmel felt a lot better after she'd washed her face and hands and changed into sweats. David had managed to remove most traces of the cellar from his clothing and hair.

She rolled up the sweatpant on her damaged side.

"Ooh," he said as he examined the wound, visibly cringing at the sight of blood. "That must hurt. Looks like you caught it on an old nail. Have you had a tetanus shot recently?"

Casting her mind back to the various scrapes and sprains and fractures she'd suffered in the past year since moving to St. Jude Without, she nodded. "Probably."

With an ancient bottle of mercurochrome long past its expiry date, he held his breath as he dabbed the bright red onto the cut knee. When the damage was covered up, he relaxed and as an afterthought, painted on a silly happy face. "There, no more tears."

His eyes crinkled with kindness again as he smiled at her. Had she imagined the impatience in his voice down in the cellar?

"Sorry," she said. "I can be a bit of a klutz sometimes."

"No, I'm the one who needs to apologize," he said, shaking his head. "I got so caught up in exploring your cellar I forgot that you were half-scared to death down there when I took the light away. Forgive me?"

He treated her with such a gaze from his gray eyes that she couldn't say no. He was an archivist, for God's sake; he probably got turned on by the old secrets of a disused cellar.

"I'm going now," Tina announced, calling attention back to herself. She stood with her arms crossed, looking disgruntled and disappointed at how the evening had turned out. What she had been expecting, Carmel couldn't begin to know, but she was glad when the door finally shut behind Tina.

"You've recovered then?"

She nodded and smiled at David.

"Great," he said, and cast his eyes up toward the ceiling and beyond. "Hmmm. I don't suppose....?"

"No!" she exclaimed, guessing what was on his mind. "No attic. I've had enough of dark places for today, thank you."

His lower lip came out rather petulantly, but he shrugged in acquiescence. "Well, I guess that's enough excitement for one night," he said. "If you're okay, then I'll head home. Mind if I use your washroom before I go?"

"Sure," she replied. "Upstairs to the right. Mind your step, and there's no overhead light in the hallway I'm afraid. But I keep a nightlight on in the bathroom, so you'll be able to find your way. Take the flashlight, just in case."

He was gone quite a long time, and she could have sworn she heard his footsteps creaking on the loose floorboards of the upstairs bedrooms before the toilet flushed. What a nosy bugger he was.

After he too had gone home, Carmel took a moment to assess the situation of Phonse's map. All was not lost. David had brushed aside her hints that she wanted to examine the old map, but she could surely wheedle his help in looking for the map, or least get him to find where it was stored in the archives. She had time, after all. She still had her job and there was no need to rush things.

Unless she got arrested for the murder, of course. There was always that possibility lurking. In which case, she needed to act fast before that happened, in order to stave that off.

Okay––so perhaps she did need to rush things after all––she needed to figure out who had the opportunity and motive to kill Marcia before she herself was arrested and charged. And she had to figure out how the map was involved, if it was involved. Could it be involved? How had she lost track of this dire need?

This kind of pressure could only be relieved by choco-late. A quick search through the cupboards showed that the silly pink boxes of the post-Valentine's sales chocolates were emptied, every one of them. Carmel had no choice but to break into the chocolate chip store in the pantry, and that stash was getting low too.

The pirate book re-appeared that night in the oddest of places. A moment after laying her head on her pillow, her neck was scratched by its hard edge.

"This is getting too weird," she said, hauling the book out from under her pillow and recognizing it even in the dim light from the moon through her window. "Really? What is Phonse doing hiding things in my bedroom? This is taking his stupid joke too far."

She threw the book across the room and let it sit where it landed, splayed open, not caring if she cracked the spine of the ancient tome. "Stupid Phonse and his stupid ghost anyway."

Things were beginning to unnerve her, even apart from having found Marcia dead in the basement archive room. And Tina––what was with that chick anyway? She was always wanting to tag along, and was really starting to creep her out now.

Chapter 16

There was another bomb scare on Monday morning, this time at the main hospital, the Health Sciences Centre, which was also part of the university. Again it was timed to create the most havoc when all the day staff were in place, day-patients in for appointments, all the many nursing, pharmacy and medicine students at their classes, and the hospital was gearing up for the week ahead. And again, it was phoned into the open line morning show.

Darrow was working with a team he was unfamiliar with, but all were well-trained in the art of bomb threats. A report was soon on his desk.

Apart from a suspicion of a slight foreign accent on the part of the muffled caller who had spread the alert of the possible bomb planted somewhere in the vast facility, there were no leads. Even after lab analysis on the voice, there was still no firm conclusion.

The HSC was a rambling hodgepodge of architecture. The initial hospital built in the '70's had been considered first rate and more than enough to serve the city for the years to come, but with the closure of older facilities and the growth of so many departments, the building's expansion had taken on a life of its own. It took hours to comb through the entire complex and to at last declare there was nary a bomb in sight.

The nuisance factor was the worst thing about this new assignment. Darrow had a lot on his plate, never mind the worry about Carmel and the looming charge, but while waiting for the officers and dogs to finish their search, his mind raced.

It was the hint of a foreign accent in the voice of the caller which brought back to mind Carmel's words last Friday. She'd said Milanovic was taking up with the independence movement. The NLA. Could that man possibly be behind the bomb threats? This was an avenue he would be very happy to pursue.

*****

As the bomb squad inspected every inch of the hospital complex on Monday morning, on the other side of town, Carmel found herself sweating in anticipation of the reception she would receive from her co-workers. After all, they weren't much used to rubbing elbows with suspected murderers. A few of the women looked at her askance when she walked in the door, but with David's acceptance, they soon thawed a little, enough to make things more comfortable for her. Just as he'd said they would do.

Even so, Tina was the only person who would actually strike up a conversation with her. She hadn't seemed bothered at all by the suspicions of murder hanging over Carmel's head, and, unlike David, hadn't even asked her how she'd fared from the experience.

Despite being mostly stuck on the front-desk, Tina seemed to know where almost everything was in the archives, so Carmel decided to enlist the younger woman's help in finding the half-map. She had to at least find out if the police had possession of it, and Tina would know. This would require a cover story in order to divert the young woman from the idea of buried treasure. Carmel was beginning to get heartily sick of the whole thing.

"You know," she began casually as she approached Tina, "that map, the one found under Water Street."

"The treasure map?" Tina asked, looking at Carmel with a light of speculation in her eyes. She tapped her long nails on the counter.

"I seriously doubt it's a treasure map; we've been through that," Carmel replied, "but the map itself, some friends of mine are interested in it."

"Why would they be interested if they didn't think it showed where Captain Jeremy buried his treasure?"

"My friends live in St. Jude Without, and they're just interested because I was told it's an early depiction of the cove," she said, praying that she sounded like she was telling the truth. Carmel knew herself to be a rotten liar. "So I just wanted to have a look at it, maybe get them a copy."

Tina nodded. "You're right; it is St. Jude Without."

Her assurance reminded Carmel of another question she had. "How can you be so certain?" she asked, momentarily diverted from her task. "You only got to peek at it over Marcia's shoulder."

Tina attempted a modest smile. "Oh, I have a photographic memory," she told her. "If I see something once, it's in my head forever."

And she probably had a mind like a steel-trap, too. Carmel was beginning to suspect that little got past Tina.

"Do they have the other half of the map?"

"What?"

"The other half," Tina reminded her. "The one Marcia received was just a half, right? I saw it; it was ripped."

"No," Carmel was able to say with the conviction of truth in her voice. "They certainly don't have the other half."

No matter that she wasn't lying, Tina still didn't seem to believe her. Her eyes narrowed with suspicion.

"You sure it's not in your house somewhere? After all, you live in Jeremy's home."

"He's been dead for two hundred years," Carmel said, sharpness slipping into her voice. "If any maps survived that time they would have been found by now."

Tina turned away from her, hurt showing in the set of her shoulders. Carmel gave a silent sigh.

"So, where would I find that map?" Carmel reminded her, in a much pleasanter voice. "Although I think Marcia had it down in the basement when... well, when she died. The police may have taken it."

"That? Oh, that's so new it won't have been processed yet. And I know it wasn't taken as evidence by the police," she said. She scrabbled around her desk and found a printout. "This is the receipt the police left for everything they took as evidence. All the folders and files that Dr. Flynn had pulled out of the shelves when she got... when she... you know."

"Shouldn't David have this list?" Carmel asked as she scanned through it.

"Well, I never had a chance to give it to him," Tina replied, sounding flustered. "I mean, there was so much going on, and unlike some people I had to stay behind and deal with everything. And help the police make this list. No one sent me home to recover from the shock."

Carmel detected a touch of resentment in Tina's tone. She needed the young woman's help so would have to stay on her good side––fortunately she knew her weaknesses.

"You know, I think I saw someone bring in a birthday cake this morning," Carmel told her. "We'll have to check that out at break time."

Tina's face brightened considerably, for she was still young enough that she'd never had to worry about cake going to her hips.

The list Tina had created was painstaking in its documentation, noting each folder found by Marcia's body with file number and––for the loose pieces of paper––a thorough description of the items. It didn't list the map in question, but was nevertheless extremely informative for Carmel. It showed that Marcia had been rifling through the old Clerkwell collection when she'd met her untimely death. The police receipt described the wills of various family members, along with bills of shipping from before the year 1800 on which Captain Jeremy Ryan's name occurred frequently.

Yet she'd had the old map with her at the time. What did Marcia know about this map of St. Jude Without? More importantly, was the map the reason she was murdered? This idea floored Carmel, but she couldn't let on to Tina the sudden surge of importance she felt that she find the map.

"You're right; it's not on this list," Carmel said. "Strange, I wonder where it went?"

"If it's not on the evidence list, it has to be here somewhere. In that case, it's probably not even in the holding cells yet," Tina replied, not questioning Carmel's interest in the dirty old piece of useless foolscap. She was used to the quirks of historians who found value in the oddest things. "Funny, there seems to have been a run on people asking for that map. I had to tell him no, as he was a member of the public. It's more than my job is worth, you know, to go letting people back there into the stacks."

"Who was looking for it?"

"Oh," Tina said with a smirk on her plain face. "This guy; he has a Ph.D. I don't think he was all that interested in the map, to tell you the truth. I think he was just using it as an excuse to chat me up." She blushed, the color adding life to her pale face. "But you work here, so it's okay. You'll probably find it in the little office off the front desk, waiting to be sorted. I'll show you when we go back."

Carmel couldn't believe it was that easy to get her hands on the map. Which, as things turned out, it wasn't.

"Strange," Tina said, making a show of rifling through all the piles. "Should be here somewhere. It can't have gotten far in that short a time."

Carmel was beginning to suspect it had gotten quite far, at least as far as the murderer had gone. "Do you think someone else might have taken it?" she asked, then hastily amended that thought. "Or borrowed it, I mean."

Tina heaved a huge sigh. "This makes my job so difficult," she said. "People take things whenever they want, and don't bother letting me know. And then when things go missing, it's all my fault. Everyone blames me."

"Who do you think would have taken it?" Carmel kept her voice low. The theory was taking hold in her mind. If she knew who had the map, then she might possibly know who the murderer was.

Tina looked around to make sure no one was listening, then leaned in to Carmel. "Well, David, for one." The sour look on her face hinted that she had something juicy to impart, but a soft noise just outside in the corridor stopped her.

"What are you looking for?" David had materialized at the open office door. He didn't look very pleased.

"Oh, David," Tina simpered, smiling up at the man who was acting head.

"Tina's just showing me around," Carmel said in a nonchalant voice.

Frankly, she was reluctant to let David know she was still looking for the map after Saturday night, for this might smell of obsession and he would want to know the whole story behind her search. She didn't want to have to explain Phonse's crazy ideas to him, because that might mark her as crazy too. She was beginning to wish Phonse had never asked her to do this.

She also needed to hold onto the nugget of suspicion about the map's role in the murder, at least until she had time to think it through.

But the boss still held Tina in his steely gaze, eyes narrowed, and she twittered on, "Carmel's looking for that old map from the Clerkwell premises," she said. "But I can't find it anywhere." She giggled again, totally inappropriately, and emboldened by his stare, dared to ask him. "Do you know where it went to?"

He glanced down at the untidy piles of papers and folders. "I don't know that we even kept that," he tossed over his shoulder as he turned away. "You might try Marcia's garbage can."

Chapter 17

That didn't sound right at all. While shelving and filing in the back room (the upstairs one this time, thank God, the one with windows) Carmel pondered about what David had said. If in fact he thought the map had been thrown away, why didn't he say so on Saturday night? There was something wrong with this picture.

Carmel knew Marcia had had the map with her just before her life had been so horribly snuffed out. It had been sitting on the table of the basement room in its Mylar film, the file folder opened as if Marcia was using it to refer to in her search through the shelves. It wasn't on Tina's painstakingly documented list, so the map hadn't been withheld by the police as evidence.

Could it still be down there? She'd knocked a lot of files off the table in her blind stumbling in the dark. Could it possibly have slipped out of its folder and gotten wedged under a shelving unit?

Drat. She knew there was only one way to find out, and the possibility had to be ruled out. Carmel had to return to the basement archive room.

She had to, but could she, in fact, physically force herself down there?

Steeling herself, she started down the back staircase before she could find reason not to, and the metal stairs clanged with each step, no matter how quietly she tried to place her feet. Carmel hadn't been down this way, of course, since the murder.

The police had finished their business now, and the corridor looked much as it always had––dimly lit and empty, with windowless doors leading off it. She turned the corner to reach the elevator and the door to the archive. There was now no doorstop waiting to keep even the bare light from the corridor shining into the basement archive room––the iron dog was in the custody of the police and had not been replaced.

She hesitated before opening the door. There was no way of telling if there was anyone inside and she didn't have a cover story ready to explain her presence. Carmel gave herself a mental shake––this was silly as she was an employee and thus could easily have business in this room.

Gritting her teeth, she opened the door to the basement archive. The fluorescent lights flashed on, humming like they'd never been off. The table was clean of files and blood, and everything looked in order. She stopped at the doorway, her heart beat slowing and her breath returning to normal.

There was nothing amiss in here, and all the stacks were well-lit. It was as if the murder had never happened, and this was just a space, a space used to store old documents. It was an innocent space, smelling of old books and cool dry air.

There was nothing here. The realization bubbled through her mind like champagne newly uncorked. She wasn't afraid.

The darbies were gone, from this space at least.

The map was also gone. A quick check of the bottom of the shelving units showed that nothing could have slipped under them, the metal was flush to the floor utilizing every single inch of storage, and the shelves were too high for someone to casually lay a file folder on top. Just to be sure, she climbed on the table and checked the upper shelves as far as she could reach. Nothing up there.

She also checked the floor of the shelves behind in case it had somehow slipped around the corner, but no luck there either. The police would have been very thorough in collecting any possible evidence.

Could the map have been accidently filed away? Carmel stopped to think, then shook her head. Everything that had been on the table would be with the police still.

But the map had disappeared, which proved to her beyond a shadow of a doubt that the map was in the possession of the murderer. Somehow this murder had to be about that old piece of paper found in a bricked up cellar under Water Street, crazy as it seemed.

"Find the map, and we've found the murderer," she whispered aloud.

The mystery had deepened, yet she left the basement with a lighter heart. Yes, she was still under suspicion of murder and she was on her own with that, no help to be looked for from the police on the case or from Darrow. But she'd conquered a bit of her claustrophobic fear, a tiny edge of it perhaps, and for that she was grateful.

Also, she'd done everything she could to look for the stupid map for Phonse and Nate, and her obligation to him was ended.

Well, she'd looked almost everywhere, she realized as she passed Marcia's office. No, it couldn't be in the garbage can, for Dr. Flynn had died before she could have brought it upstairs, and it was definitely on the table in the basement when Carmel had last seen it.

A quick peek, just to assure herself, and she darted in through the open door.

There was a lot of paper in the dented metal bin, but a quick shuffle through it showed that she was right; the map was not there.

"What..." asked a cold voice, "what are you doing here?"

She looked up from the bin to see David looking down at her, with Tina peering around him, her mouth agape. David's eyes glittered like the sun behind the silver thaw on a February morning. This was not the David who had comforted her and drawn a happy face on her knee.

Carmel straightened up immediately, her brown curls shaking. "Sorry, David," she said. "I shouldn't be in this room, I know, I just thought I'd..."

What was she planning to say, that she'd turned custodian and was going to empty the bin? She had no business in this office and they both knew it.

David's face was showing a struggle between whatever had set him off and the realization that his reaction was inappropriate. His civility won out. "Did you find what you're looking for?" He tried to say it lightly, but there was still a horrible suspicion haunting those gray eyes.

She hated that stare for she didn't know what he was accusing her of.

The tension between them was broken as Tina spoke up.

"Coffee break time!" she sang. "There's cheesecake from Manna Bakery; you don't want to miss it!"

Carmel looked back up to David and shrugged. "Cheesecake," she mumbled, happy for an excuse to dash away from the confusion and uncomfortable feelings left from their exchange.

Chapter 18

This was a half-day for Carmel so she was free to leave at 12:30, having successfully avoided David for the rest of the morning. Or was he avoiding her?

She also didn't answer her phone when Phonse called looking for an update on the old map.

She needed thinking time, a space to get away from David's oddness and the other weirdnesses in her life. Phonse's latest bee in his bonnet, his plan to strike it rich and the subsequent pressure he was putting on her as solely responsible for his happiness, it was all too much, especially as she knew it was solely to benefit Nate.

Phonse had a bit of a man-crush on Nate, she suspected, not that she would point this out to him. He followed his younger relative around like a big Labrador puppy, agreeing with everything the educated man said and taking on his mannerisms and talk. Phonse was not a political animal by nature, and it didn't sit right hearing him spout independence and the need for self-governance.

She shuddered to think what would happen if men like Nate were in charge of the place.

Carmel needed a good long walk where she could get away from all these men who were crowding her head. The lake was still full of ice and mud, so she got in her car and headed over to Cape Spear, twenty minutes down the shore. This most easterly point in North America, the spit of rock scraped bare by the ocean ice still had a working lighthouse that sent a beacon to warn passing ships of the rocks which lurked just under the water. Don't come near! the single beam flashed.

A person could breathe out here in the clean salt air, all sins and anxieties whipped clean by the wind, standing at the lookout, watching the gray waves wash the rocks. An early iceberg floated far out in the ocean, way too early in the season. You could see for miles here.

Kicking around the crumbling concrete war bunkers, her mind wandered, as minds do when presented with the vastness of the ocean on all sides and little else to catch the eye.

Jealousy. Dani was jealous, Darrow's daughter. Jealous that she might lose the star spot of being the only female in his life, so cutting their one evening together short. And the fifteen-year-old's insecurity was totally understandable, having been abandoned by her other parent. Carmel knew all about being abandoned by parents.

Well, the kid got her wishes. The chasm between herself and Darrow was so wide now it looked to be insurmountable. Dani had her dad all to herself, and good luck with that.

And professional jealousy. Dr. Taverstock was at the head of his profession as was Marcia, both reigning over the long history of the former colony. There were lots of stories told about the ancient fights between the two, territorial quibbles and verbal battles enacted between the stacks.

Could he have murdered Marcia? He'd had the opportunity that day, having been given license to move around the back spaces as he chose, and he had also been seen running out with his overcoat already on. She wished she could have witnessed it, seen if he'd had his gray smock on underneath or if it was balled up in his pocket, hiding the bloody evidence.

But wait––Laney had said the cover-all was found in the washroom. Surely he wouldn't have left that item behind––Tony's gray smock was his trademark, and was sure to be covered with years of his ground-in DNA. They would have arrested him already if anyone suspected it was his.

And what reason would the librarian have, seriously? He had no motive that she could think of. Then again, she didn't know the man.

David? Could David be jealous of Marcia and impatient for her to retire so he could move up the ladder? She almost laughed to think about it. David Clerkwell came from old money and didn't even have to work, especially not in the low paying field of cultural heritage. She was pretty sure David worked there only for the love of old documents.

And from what she knew of David, Carmel doubted if he would have the stomach for violent murder. Poisoning perhaps, or snipe shooting from a distance where he didn't have to see the bloody gore, that would be more his style. He had been throwing his guts up just at the sight of the blood the day of Marcia's murder, and she remembered how he'd winced at the sight of her knee and had to force himself to minister to her.

There was also another kind of jealousy, the islanders' jealousy of outsiders, of CFA's. Like Nate O'Reilly and his fury that he couldn't get a job at the university despite his PhD in a subject at the heart of Newfoundland's past, colonial history.

She stopped short, not seeing the seagulls fly in the wind or the huge ships bringing supplies out to the oilfields away over the horizon, for she was seeing pieces fall into place in her mind.

Nate claimed to know The Rooms and the archives department like the back of his hand, knowing all the hiding places from where to avoid work, or to slip out and smoke his cigarettes during working hours. He would know how to slink past the loosely guarded gates, and he would know which doors were kept propped open. He would know where the fire doors led to for a quick getaway. And the fact that the cameras were never hooked up.

Nate had many chips on his shoulder born of per-ceived past injustices, including being fired by Marcia all those years ago.

Phonse was trying to get the map for Nate's sake, as a surprise for him, like a lover bringing his sweetheart her heart's desire. But perhaps Phonse didn't know that Nate already had the map? Perhaps Nate had stolen it from under Marcia's dying body after he'd bashed in her head with the iron dog.

Nate had known that Marcia had the old map from the Clerkwell premises––Carmel herself had told him.

Which meant the murder was definitely about the map. Her suspicions had been correct.

Oh Lord. She found herself reaching into her pocket for her phone to call Darrow. Yes, she knew she wasn't supposed to call him or contact him in any way or bridge that chasm until she was no longer considered a suspect in Marcia's death, even if he was no longer on the case. By rights, she should be getting in touch with Evelyn Wright.

But Darrow was the only one she had on speed dial.

Chapter 19

Meanwhile that afternoon, Darrow was chasing his own demon in the form of Ruscan Milanovic. He'd had plenty of time to let his Saturday night thoughts dwell and multiply in his mind over the weekend, even with the distractions of the petty squabbles with Danielle and all the thousand demands of two teenagers. Laney was set on proving that Carmel was a murderer and Darrow was just as set on proving the man wrong. Perhaps he was grasping at straws in an attempt to clear Carmel's name, or perhaps it was his own dislike of Laney that was driving him.

And perhaps he couldn't see that he was losing perspective, but he now had the bomb scares and Milanovic's possible involvement with the NLA. This gave him a legitimate excuse for hounding the man, which he fully intended to do.

He drove through the downtown streets of Duckworth, Water and Harbour Drive, scanning every illegal parking spot, but he found no sign of the chip van. He finally found it parked at the bottom of Temperance Street near to where the old rusted trawler rocked against the pier, right at the end of Water Street. By rights, Darrow should have a constable with him, someone as back-up and witness, but he had a feeling that what he wanted to do should not be witnessed.

Rotted tires attached as buffers on the wharf creaked as they rubbed against the metal hull, the only sound down here at the far eastern edge of the harbor, and Darrow felt totally alone. Not even the seagulls were present today, squawking at each other as they fought for the choice bits from the sewage outlet fifty feet out into the harbor.

This was the forgotten end of the St. John's harbor, desolate by day. It sprang to life only in the dark hours when the squatters and rats who shared the abandoned stone houses of Temperance Street came out to look for sustenance while the rent-boys plied their trade to nondescript minivans trawling under the streetlights.

A chill wind from the ocean cut through him as he crunched his way over the icy landscape to the wooden pier. The flimsy cat walk leading up to the hulk swayed under his weight and the smell of rust, salt and fish pervaded the old wreck.

"Milanovic!" he called through the first doorway he came to. It opened into a dingy metal corridor which stretched through the heart of the ship and his voice echoed back at him from deep inside the bowels of the boat. The cold emanated from inside the iron hull on this sunny day. There was no way the Ukrainian could not have heard him in the stillness.

He walked along the slippery deck, the paint-chipped rail cold beneath his gloves. The few windows of the ship were burred with salt and dirt––rubbing at one, he found there was little enough to see inside, and still no signs of life. All the other doorways were locked or frozen tight.

As Darrow rounded the boat back to the gangway, he looked down at the pier and noticed for the first time the single set of footprints leading away from the boat. They were iced over, the sun reflecting off the raised edges and some windblown snow had blurred their corners. Milanovic was long since gone.

"Damn it!"

It was the pain of the unyielding iron rail as his hands beat on it that brought him back to his senses. What was he playing at, being a lone vigilante in the search to clear his girlfriend's name? Did he think he was some kind of knight in shining armor? Right now he saw that he was Don Quixote jousting with windmills, an idealistic fool. If Darrow was one of his own subordinates, he would have had choice words for the officer. As it was he could only direct them at himself. Allowing his personal life to impinge on his professionalism––now that made him even more angry at himself.

***

Carmel stopped on the high road leading down into Shea Heights, on top of the brow which overlooked the city sparkling far below. From this vantage point, she could see the hills and cliff tops far beyond St. John's, framed by the spruce woods to her left and to her right, the far hills blue and white in the clear morning sun with Cabot Tower glinting golden in the foreground. The wind buffeted the small blue car as she waited for him to answer.

"Look, I know I'm not supposed to contact you," she said in a rush as she heard Darrow's voice on the phone. "But the map––it's missing."

The reception wasn't the best way up here and she could barely make out his words through the gusts of static.

"I know it's not your case," she said, "but I don't have anyone else to turn to!"

A breaking burst of Darrow's voice told her he wasn't pleased by something.

"Just listen to me, will you?" Her voice was rising to make him hear. "The map from the old Clerkwell property––it's missing. I saw it just before Marcia got killed; she had it on the table but now it's nowhere to be found."

She took the phone away from her ear in a slow movement. "I can't believe he hung up on me," she said aloud to the single crow perched on the wires above, gripping on in the wind. "None of his business indeed."

Carmel put the car in gear and jumped the clutch while she did so. "Phonse wasn't so far off the mark," she continued, her face set and grim. "Lov'em and leav'em at the first sign of trouble? He can't be unprofessional––I have to discuss my worries with Laney? Right, the guy who wants to lock me away just to make his life easier."

She sped through the thirty kilometer an hour zone leading into the heart of the small community without it even registering and she continued down the hill, screeching her tires as she took the dangerous curve at the foot.

***

"What do you mean you lost the map?"

She'd never seen Phonse this angry before. He loomed over her in the kitchen of the old cottage, blond-gray curls like a halo against the overhead light and face in a scowl. His fists were raised and clenched, and she found herself cowering back against the counter, freshly filled kettle in her hand.

"Stop it, Phonse! You're scaring me." Their eyes locked. He saw her fear, and slowly brought his fists back down to his sides, turning away.

"I can't believe you lost my map," he said, a whine replacing the anger in his voice as he swung out the old wooden chair and sat himself at the table. "That was my future, and you threw it away."

"I didn't lose your stupid map," she replied. "I never had it to begin with."

"You were the last one to see it," he pointed out, head in his hands. "What am I going to tell Nate now?"

"What do you mean?"

"You know this was going to be a surprise for Nate," he told her as he slipped further down and laid his head on his arms. His voice was muffled by the scarred oak table. "He was talking about the old legends, and the map, and I was going to get it for him and..."

"And what? You'd be best buds forever?" She couldn't help the sharp nasty tang in her voice. Phonse and his man-crush. Carmel turned the stove on and placed the filled kettle on the burner.

"What do you know about anything?" he asked as he lifted his head. "This is our heritage. It's not yours, so you don't understand."

"Rub it in, why don't you?" she retorted. "I'm not from here, and I don't belong in the cove. Go ahead, say it. I don't belong anywhere; I'm not one of you guys."

"Oh, Carmel," he said, jumping up to put his arms around her. "Come off it, don't be like that. That's not what I'm saying at all. Where'd you get that idea from?"

He wore an army issue flak jacket over his white t-shirt. The soft cotton was warm to her hands, and she breathed in the familiar smell of Phonse, the smell of salt and sweat and cigarette smoke.

She could feel the hot spurt of tears behind her eyes at this display of niceness and sympathy from such an unexpected source and sniffed them back. "It's just, it's been all so horrible," she said into his shoulder, her voice catching. "First Marcia and that basement and the... the blood, and everyone thinks I did it, and then John won't even speak to me..."

"Who's John?" Phonse broke in, holding her away from him.

"Darrow," she replied, dabbing her nose with her sleeve.

"I told you not to bother with him. He's a cop––don't you know never to trust a cop?" He gave a small laugh, a kind one meant to jolly her out of her tears. "For sure you're not from the cove if you haven't learned that yet."

The kettle began its whistle and she poured it into the waiting pot.

"Isn't there any beer on offer here?"

"No," she said. "I've gained ten pounds since Christmas, and it's all from beer and bar snacks. You're having chamomile tea."

He sniffed at the cup she poured with a grimace. "Gross," he said. He hauled out a small flask from one of the many pockets of his light jacket and poured a healthy dose into the cup. "Want some? It's London Dock."

"It's got just as many calories in it, probably more because it's made from sugar," she objected.

"So go for a walk tomorrow," he said. "Or come help me out on the boat; do some real work."

She shrugged as he poured rum into her cup. A hot toddy never hurt, did it?

"So," she said, her mind harking back to something he'd said. "You said Nate doesn't know you're looking for the map?"

Phonse shook his head. "No," he said. "But he always used to talk about that story, you know? That was one of the legends which he was fixated on ever since he was little. He's got plans for the money that treasure would bring into the cove."

"Like what?" Carmel took a first sip of the hot sweet beverage. The rum was strong, overpowering the delicate flower taste of the tea.

He looked up with fire in his eyes. "Nate's going to set himself up in politics," he said. "Nate's going to take on the big guys, and make Newfoundland independent again."

She said nothing, not wanting to get into a dumb argument about the feasibility of this plan. This land was full of dreamers and artists, that was part of its charm, but few of them were very practical. You didn't want them captaining a ship, let alone the province.

"He'd do anything to help us all out," Phonse said earnestly. "He's a leader."

Anything. Perhaps Nate didn't know that Phonse was looking for the map, or that he'd planned this surprise. Carmel had the uncomfortable feeling that Nate might already have the map in his possession. How to tell Phonse this?

"Has Nate been after you to get the map?" she asked.

Phonse looked up. "No," he said, as he cocked his head in thought. "Funny that, considering how gung-ho he's always been to find the treasure." He laughed. "Maybe he's trying to get it for himself. He'll be shocked when I show up with it!"

"The map's gone missing, remember?"

"Oh, right," Phonse said.

She remembered what she'd been meaning to ask Phonse.

"Do you know Ruscan?"

"Who? Rusty? Never heard of him."

"Uh uh," she said. "Ruscan. He's a foreigner. I was wondering if he's been hanging around with you guys, with Nate."

"No. Should I know him?"

"I just wondered, because he said he was involved with the liberation movement," Carmel said.

"Is he the t-shirt guy?" Phonse asked. "British dude, with dreads?"

"No, that's not him. Never mind," Carmel said. She had to word her next question very carefully. "Has Nate ever been, I don't know, violent?"

Phonse barked with laughter. "Nate? No, geez, he's a real softie," he said. "He went to university. He reads books––he can't even go hunting in the fall, can't stand having to lug the dead moose back out over the barrens."

"Still," Carmel continued, "you said he'd do anything. And that he's been fixated on the map his whole life." She would have to tread very carefully here, even with the rum going straight to her head.

Her companion grew still. "I hope you're not going where I think you're going," he said.

She set the cup down in its saucer. "Could he have murdered Marcia over this map?"

"Ah, geez, Carmel," Phonse said, wincing as he did so. "Come off it. He's not going to kill for it, you know, we're not still in the age of pirates."

"Really? Well, what's the Newfoundland Liberation Army all about then?" she flashed back at him. She took another swallow of hot rum. It really wasn't so awful after the first sip deadened the taste buds.

"It's not an army, like that," Phonse said. "It's... it's more of a concept. Besides, the archives are locked. You said you could only get down to the basement room through the front desk. Did anyone see Nate there that day?"

Carmel thought about that day, and the people who were in the reading room.

"Phonse, don't you remember driving us both to town that day?"

He paused, the cup half way to his mouth. "Oh, that was that day? I dropped Nate off at the coffee shop."

"Yes," Carmel said, "and then he was there in the public room of the archives. I avoided speaking to him."

"So he was there!" Phonse said, shocked now. "But still––I thought you said no one could get past the gate into the basement––wasn't that where the woman was killed? You said Nate was in the public room."

Carmel nodded. "But Nate knows his way around there pretty well, doesn't he? He was boasting about that, in fact, just the other night. The first time I met him."

Phonse didn't answer, but started shaking his head.

"He knows the Archives; he said he used to work there," she argued. "He would know how to get in through the back way if anybody did."

"I think," said Phonse. "I think you're tired and drunk. This is Nate we're talking about! I've known him all his life. He's full of hot air sometimes, but he's no killer."

"But..."

"Change the subject," Phonse said, holding up his hand. He refused to listen to her.

"Well, he..."

"Stop! No more," Phonse said. He topped up both their cups, emptying the flask. "Not even going to consider this. Hey, how's Captain Jem––you met him yet?"

"Oh, Phonse," Carmel said. "No, I have not met your stupid ghost, and I don't really want to, thank you very much." She threw back the entire contents of the cup in one big gulp, and almost coughed as it burned down her throat. "Whoa, that's even stronger."

"Yeah," Phonse agreed after finishing his own cupful. "100 proof rum, you can't beat it."

"Is that stuff even legal?" She gazed about her, realizing she was seeing double. She squeezed her eyes together to help them focus.

"Depends where you are," he said, standing up to go, not even swaying with the strong drink inside him. It took years to build a tolerance like that. "In St. Pierre it's legal."

The tiny islands just to the south of Newfoundland still belonged to France, probably the last colonies in the Western Hemisphere, and booze was cheap down there. Carmel suspected that Phonse and Sid made a couple of quiet journeys down there each year, but the less said about that the better.

"And listen," Phonse said as he paused before heading out the door, "there's no way that Nate is the killer. You need to get that out of your head right now. Depend on it."

Carmel couldn't tell if he were trying to convince her or himself that Nate was innocent of murder.

She locked the front door behind Phonse for the wind was rising outside. The forecasts were calling for Force 2 hurricane winds that night, an unexpected meeting of systems way out over the Atlantic Ocean to the east and there would be power outages along with it––that would be a certainty. This was weather more suited to the fall, not the late winter. If it snowed, there would be blizzard conditions, but the night was mercifully clear. She watched a moment as clouds scudded across the full moon and much closer, the lilac bush was scraping against the side of the house. The wind was rising.

Chapter 20

She left the rum-soaked cups in the sink to be dealt with the next day. Switching off the kitchen light as she prepared to turn in for the night, she glanced out the window into the backyard and trees and graveyard beyond. The full moon lit the snow and she could pick out each branch lined in silver. There were no dancing lights tonight. She hadn't seen them since the end of December, just before the winter snows arrived.

Did fairies hibernate? If they existed, that is. In the spring, she could explore this more thoroughly, but right now Carmel's mind was feeling sozzled with Phonse's London Dock and she just wanted to fall into sleep to get away from it all. The murder, the charges pending against her, the stupid map––all of it.

Despite her intentions, she dreamed of Captain Jem that night. In this dream, she herself was looking out her bedroom window, and it was a moonlit night just like tonight, the moon now off towards the western horizon. The old pirate was standing on the point, way down there where the ponies grazed even now in the dead of winter, but it wasn't the point, it was a different landscape somehow. And he was looking at her, she knew, and shaking his head, she could tell by the feather, nodding and waving in the wind.

And the wind was continuing to rise. In the space between sleep and dreams, she could hear it whistling through the chimney next to her head and through the cracks and crevices of the old wooden cottage and through the chinks in the stone foundation. Outside in the cove, the searching wind wrapped itself round deck chairs left forgotten in the winter and the remnants of Christmas lights tacked along the edges of the houses, and it pulled its hardest to rip them all away only to fling them away again unsatisfied. It found the loose shutters on Clyde's old farmhouse and fought with them; it took Phonse's lobster pots from the wharf and cast them onto the water.

The only thing the wind couldn't wrench away were the boulders laying by the road and the icicles clinging to the sides of the mountain and the ravine.

From that space, Carmel woke for a moment, caught by the sound of movement above her head, a slow shuffle of wood on wood, dragged along the bare floorboards.

"Phonse," she groaned into her pillow, still half-asleep, "you never fixed my roof." He'd stuck a piece of plywood over the hole in her roof last summer on a fine August day, and had never gone back to repair the damage. The wind must have found its way in there. She didn't want to dwell on the havoc she would find up there in the small attic space, and if she woke up for real, she would have no choice but to go up and check it out. She turned over and disappeared into her dreams again.

It was the light that first alerted her, dragging her body consciousness back from wherever she was, the faint light on her eyelids like the touch of the earliest dawn, and her eyes opening that brought her fully back to the here and now. A faint muffled glow at her doorway.

Was this the fairies come in out of the cold? Or was it worse?

Yes, it was far worse. This must be the old hag, the one who came upon sleeping bodies in the dead of night and sat on them, paralysing them with her dread intent. Carmel knew her well, and she knew from experience that the only way to break the spell was to force her body and soul to act together in an almighty roar and banish the hag back to whence she'd sprung.

Yet she lay in her bed unable to move. It's just a dream, she told herself. The old hag doesn't exist. Don't panic.

But then the light flashed in her pupils which were still relaxed with sleep, blinding her and leaving the after image solid on her retinas. She sensed rather than saw the tall shape reaching out towards her, and then she found she could move, she could scream!

And so she did. She screamed and screamed, one part of her mind amazed that she was victorious over the old hag, while another part watched the figure grab something from her bedside table then disappear, light and all. She screamed so loud she didn't hear the light footsteps pattering down the stairs and the front door unlocked and opened, left to bang in the wind.

She only stopped when she heard the car start outside and move away fast, very fast, way too fast on the narrow gravel road with its cliff side turns around the solid granite of the mountain.

Still disbelieving that this had been real and not a nightmare, Carmel made her slow way to the window. There she stood above the cove, much as she had during her dream of Captain Jem, and watched as red tail lights disappeared, swallowed up by the mountain bend, only to reappear seconds later above Snellen's Field for a short moment while the back wheels fishtailed on the icy ruts, then they were lost to her sight.

The moon was gone now, there was no light save the glow reflected on the water from the wharf on Portugal Cove in the distance to the south, beyond the mountain. Yet even without the moonlight, she could see the white of the ocean's waves as they smashed into the shore, driven on by this crazy wild wind. Far across the water on Bell Island, she caught a series of bright blue flashes, like a string of lightning beads. Their power lines were falling, one by one.

Carmel returned to her bed, unsure whether to huddle back into its warmth or to act. She thought she should phone the police as her house had just been broken into. The phone was on her bedside table, along with the lamp. She switched on the lamp.

She did have power, unlike Bell Island across the water, but Captain Jem's pirate book was no longer there.

Phone in her hand, she automatically hit Darrow's number, then caught herself. Not Darrow, he would just be mad again if she called him, especially in the middle of the night.

911 then? But it was no longer an emergency, surely, the man (or woman, but not the old hag of her nightmares) had gotten away and was no longer a threat. Were you allowed to call if it was no longer a matter of life and death?

Her finger hovered over Phonse's contact. But he was always complaining that he was the one who had to save her, get her out of sticky situations, drive her to the hospital. Best not. Besides, he was still sore at her too for letting the map disappear. God knows what he would say if he found out about the book being stolen.

Had her intruder really stolen the old pirate book?

"Oh my God," she said aloud. "Did this even happen?" She glanced again at the table beside her. Yes, the book was missing. A quick check under the bed showed it hadn't fallen there, the dust down there hadn't been disturbed in months. The book was gone.

Evelyn Wright had given her a card number with her contact number before she'd left the police station after that horrible gruelling interview with Laney. But that was about Marcia's death, not for a routine police call for a break-in.

It was almost too much to think about and it wasn't till she noticed her feet were freezing did she accept that it was real. The culprit hadn't closed the front door in his haste to get away, and the wind had stolen whatever heat the old house held.

Chapter 21

B y the time the two RNC constables arrived through the gale to St. Jude Without, Carmel was huddled in her blankets at the kitchen table, having shut and locked the front door, cranked up the heat and made a hot sweet cup of tea.

It was Constable Brown of the wide intelligent eyes who sat across from her, listening to her story with the greatest of sympathy.

"Have you checked all around the house to see if anything else is missing?"

"No," Carmel said. "There's not much here to steal." They both looked around at the kitchen which looked even dingier in the harsh overhead light. Her only TV sat on the counter top, an ancient black and white which had been top of the line back in the nineteen-eighties. Her stereo was a boom-box of similar vintage purchased from a garage sale for five bucks. The constable was standing by the sink where the dirty cups had been left to mature overnight, and she sniffed the air suspiciously.

Carmel hastily guided her out of the kitchen and the two went through the entire house, checking out what little jewelry was in the box. Everything was present and accounted for.

Constable Brown's eyes lit up for a moment when she walked into the living room, until Carmel assured her this was a normal mess, not the result of a thief rifling through her belongings.

"Any idea how he could have gained entrance?" Brown was now asking her. "I notice the back door's unlocked. Is that usual?"

Carmel nodded. When you lived around the bay, even in a small cove like this so close to the city, no one ever thought about locking the door. Phonse used to make fun of her for securing the front door, but she only ever did that to keep the old door from blowing open in the wind.

"Well," said Brown, "since it wasn't technically a forced entry, and nothing was stolen other than a book, I'm not going to get the scene of crime team out here; that can wait till tomorrow morning. And you didn't catch any details about the car you saw speeding away?"

Carmel shook her head. It could have been any make of vehicle on that dark night. All she'd seen were red tail lights going past Snellen's Field.

The male constable accompanying Brown had done a thorough search of the house, even the attic where she had first heard sounds and assured her there was no one else present.

"You're leaving?" Carmel watched as the two officers gathered their things.

It was hard to miss the pity in the constable's blue eyes. "You're still in shock," she told her. "Is there someone you can call to be with you?"

The only person she really wanted by her side right now was Darrow, but that was out of the question. He had distinctly told her not to contact him, not while she was still a suspect for Marcia's murder and he had made that all too excruciatingly clear. Carmel shook her head. "I'll be okay."

The constable hesitated at the door as if she wanted to say more−−professionalism and humanity battling for precedence in her eyes. She saw a lot, despite her youth, and understood the heart. "I'll let Inspector Darrow know about this, if you like," she said in a low voice, "tomorrow morning."

Hope sparked with Carmel, only to flare down immediately. "No, that's all right," she said. "Best not to mention it." She couldn't take the disappointment if he did nothing. Couldn't bear that one bit.

It was pointless trying to sleep that night, so she turned on all the lights in the house and huddled in the living room, drinking cup after cup of tea. Where was the neighborhood watch when she needed them? The neighbors were quick enough to spot when a strange man's car was parked in her driveway, but had no one seen the police car and all the lights on and thought she might need assistance? Her life had turned into a nightmare.

It had all begun with the chest found in the cellar deep under Water Street. The chest with its old clothing, the skeleton of a murdered man and the map. Or to be correct, the half-map.

That map had been on the table just before Marcia was so brutally murdered, the map which had supposedly belonged to Captain Jem who built this very house and established the community of St. Jude Without two hundred years ago. And then the map had since disappeared. It was all about the map——it had to be, and Carmel was on her own in this one. And her freedom might depend on it.

Darrow had told her it was a rough sketch of St. Jude Without, but without the houses and the roads. He'd also said the word 'fairies' was the single bit of script on the paper. It had to be referring to the fairies purported to live behind her house in the old graveyard. But what of them? It was undoubtedly Captain Jeremy's map, but it couldn't be a treasure map, for there was no 'X' to mark that spot. Nothing to represent at all where the dowry was buried, if that's what the map's purpose even was.

Had he buried the treasure in the graveyard?

If Captain Jeremy hadn't buried Eliza's dowry here in St. Jude Without, then where? It could be anywhere along the thousands of kilometers of coast line on the island. It could even be in Bermuda where he'd based his operations in the early years of turning pirate.

Carmel looked around the room, lit still by the harsh overhead bulb and both the lamps, and felt a slight embarrassment that the constables had seen her customary disorder. Having a largish house meant never having to put stuff away until company was expected, and that included discarded socks and sweaters and last night's supper dishes. Gross. She could see every particle of dust——and worse, every spot where the dust had been disturbed.

Being awake late in the night to the early morning was like having bonus time, like winning the time lottery, and she put it to good use by giving the house a thorough dusting and vacuuming. And it kept her mind off the nightmare she'd just lived through.

By the time she made it upstairs, though, the dawn was breaking and her energy was flagging. Still, remembering the layer of dust under the bed gave her impetus to keep going.

She found the piece of paper when she was chasing dust bunnies from under the bureau in her bedroom. Carmel moved the dresser out of the way and the old piece of linen paper was lying underneath. Unlike the floor beneath it, the map was dust free.

"It must have come out of the pirate book," she said, remembering how she'd flung the old book across the room in a fit of childish pique.

She sat on the unmade bed and studied it, drawing the quilt over her shoulders as she realized what she had in her hands. This was a map, and it was old, yet it was of no place that she could recognize.

If it came from Captain Jem's book, then perhaps it was a map drawn from the pirate's own hand. But it wasn't a map of any recognizable place, nowhere that she could see even though she looked at it from every angle.

The lines were of faded brown ink, showing a small pond by the water's edge and a rock structure that looked like a dog. A Newfoundland dog, from what she could tell by the rough drawing.

She turned it around and squinted to make out the writing.

Under the dog which guards ...

Which guards what? And where? There was a very fancy 'X' by the dog statue, or rock formation, or whatever it was. Was that an 'X' to mark the spot of a pirate's treasure?

Was this where Eliza's dowry was buried? But where was the location described by the map?

There was something about the shape of the paper that caught at her, and after studying the edges for a moment, she realized that one of them was slightly off center, not true. The ink of the drawing ran right to the end of this page, as did the words. The original map had been ripped in half.

"Oh my God!" The ink and the hand looked similar to the other map, the one that had appeared when the whole business had started. This was the other half of the map found under Water Street! That meant that Carmel held the key to the missing map, right here in her hand.

She turned off the lights in the house. It was still too early to call anyone, even though the sun's rays were now hitting the cliffs of Bell Island across the tickle and the day was bright outside. And besides--who was there to call?

Not Phonse, for he would want to pass the map on to Nate. And Nate was the contender for the murder of Marcia, in her books. Nate, with his need for money to finance his political pipe-dreams, and who may already have killed to get hold of the other half of the map. No way was she going to let it fall into his soiled hands.

David was the map expert. She'd ask David what he thought of it. Carmel wasn't due in for work that day, but he would be there.

Jumping up from the bed, she caught a look at herself in the antique mirror over the dresser. It wasn't just the speckled glass that made her look like a wild woman. Her hair was a matted mess, with suspicions of cobwebs dangling from the flattened bit over her left ear. And it wasn't just last night's mascara that caused the dark shadows under her eyes, but no doubt it contributed. She looked worse than Melba, the witch next door, on her maddest days.

Okay, a shower first before venturing out into public, something to mend the ravages caused by the lack of sleep last night.

Carmel stood under the hot spray for longer than usual, scrubbing every inch of her, washing off the horror which still lurked in her mind from last night. It soothed her and helped bring back a semblance of normality.

Wrapped only in her short terry dressing gown with fresh thick wool socks on her feet, the coffee was dripping along nicely when she heard the knock at her front door and a deep voice calling her name.

It was Darrow standing there, the concern in his warm brown eyes turning to relief when he saw her apparently well and in one piece. His arms enveloped her and hugged her close, his open overcoat surrounding her. She took a deep breath of his smell of citrus and dark spice, laying her head against his shoulder and delighting in the sensation.

"You're alright then?" he asked and hugged her closer. "Why did you not call me? I came as soon as I found out." His Scots accent overrode the scolding of his words.

She did not answer, but drew him inside the house and shut the door.

"It's still chilly outside," she said. "I guess Constable Brown told you. I did ask her not to." Not that she minded one bit.

They went into the kitchen where Carmel poured up coffees for them both and gave him the details of the break-in.

"You didn't have your back door locked?" Darrow was incredulous.

Carmel ignored this––he was a cop, and not from the province. He wouldn't understand about unlocked doors in a small community like this. "All the person took was a book," she said. "An old book about pirates. So no big loss. All that happened was I got a great big scare."

"It could have been much worse," he scolded her.

"But it wasn't," she insisted. "I'm okay now."

She paused. Darrow hadn't been interested in the map before, but the break-in and theft of the old book might change that. "About the book..." she began.

"Was it valuable?" he asked.

Carmel shook her head. "I don't think so," she said. "But the person might not have been after the book itself. Hang on a minute."

She ran back up over the stairs and retrieved the map from her bed.

"I think this came out of the book a couple of days ago," she said. "I found it in my bedroom this morning after the break-in."

He squinted at the map, holding it out a distance to see it better. On hearing the news of her break-in, he'd left the house in such a hurry he'd forgotten his reading glasses. "It's a map of some sort," he said. "Do you know it?"

She nodded. "You're right, it's a map. But do you see that edge there? It looks like it's been torn."

"Yes, I see that," he said. "But why are you so excited about it?"

"This may be connected to the other map, the map in the chest with the skeleton––remember? I think it's important," she said. "And I think whoever murdered Marcia, came to my house last night looking for the rest of it. And I think I know who it is."

He looked incredulous. "Murdering over a map? It's a bit far-fetched."

"You don't understand," she said. "It may be a treasure map. Nate O'Reilly probably knows..."

She was interrupted in her explanation by loud thumping on the door.

"Oh, no, I forgot," she said, her hands flying to her mouth. "That's probably the scene of crime team coming to get evidence. Constable Brown said they'd be along this morning."

They stared at each other for a brief moment. Carmel was still under suspicion of murdering Dr. Flynn, and Inspector Darrow should not be seen anywhere near her home, especially by other officers of the RNC.

"Do you want to slip out the back door?" she whispered.

He shook his head. "They'll have seen my car already," he said. "I'm not the investigating officer in the murder, and they'll quite understand that I've only come to visit you out of concern. Go ahead, let them in."

But it wasn't the Scene of Crime Team, not that early in the morning. On the doorstep stood Inspector Laney, his eyes still puffy from nameless indulgences of the previous night, but yet holding the light of triumph within.

Chapter 22

In the chill of the open door, Carmel became aware she was wearing only a short robe. Laney's victorious eyes traveled down the length of her body.

"Entertaining, are we?" he said with a leer in his voice. "Sorry to have to cut the visit short." He pushed his way through the door and past her, into the kitchen where Darrow now stood by his chair, empty coffee cup before him.

"Hey, John, fancy seeing you here," she heard Laney laugh, but there was meanness in his voice. "The morning after, eh? Hope it was a good one, because there ain't going to be any more for quite a long time. I'll take over from here."

Carmel was left at the open door staring with consternation at Evelyn Wright. The sergeant met her eyes with an unreadable look, one that hinted of accusation with an overtone of anger in the set of her eyebrows, but the female officer said nothing.

"Best come in," Carmel said, allowing Wright and the other officer in.

"Constable Dickson, you got the cuffs?" Laney asked. "Carmel McAlistair, we're here to arrest you for the murder of Dr. Marcia Flynn. Read her the rights, Dickson."

"There's no need of this!" Darrow's voice was thunderous.

Constable Dickson ignored his outburst and continued on with his recitation before reaching for Carmel's hands.

"Don't be bloody ridiculous! You've no evidence for the murder." Darrow's professional composure was completely lost.

"Perhaps we could allow Ms. McAlistair to get dressed first," Evelyn cut in with her calm voice. "And you should pack a small bag," she said to the other woman. "Just in case."

"You're not serious, surely," she said to Laney, hardly able to form the words. He was a scary man and it took a lot of guts for her to speak out. She looked at Darrow then Wright, beseeching them both.

Laney paused, then gave assent with a flick of head. "Hurry up about it. We haven't got all day."

As she fled up the stairs she could hear the raised voices from below, the two Inspectors of the RNC finally battling out years of confrontation which had only ever before taken the form of snide looks and terse orders. She couldn't listen.

She reappeared in the kitchen with a hastily packed overnight bag. Carmel couldn't even remember what she'd placed in it.

The standoff between the two men had died down, at least verbally, Darrow having gotten a firm grip on himself again. She stopped, hesitating, in the doorway.

He looked over at her with leftover rage still in his eyes. "You'd best go with him," he said, fighting for control in his voice as he tried to reassure her. "We'll get this straightened out."

As Constable Dickson jangled the hand-cuffs, Darrow silenced him with a look, and the cuffs disappeared back into his overcoat pocket after an apologetic look at Laney. He led Carmel out to the door where for the first time she saw the police car drawn up outside with its red white and blue lights flashing.

This had drawn the attention of the entire cove, of course, and the inhabitants were out en masse to watch. There was Vee Ryan at the head of the lane, hair in rollers with a scarf over them against the cold, shaking her head and muttering to Marge, her carbon copy neighbor. Grouchy Clyde Farrell the farmer and his large black dog stood down the road by the bridge, alert, to make sure the police didn't try to trespass on his property. Even Melba, her neighbor through the trees was there, speechless at the sight of Carmel being led into the waiting police car.

Phonse and Nate stood not far away, looks of resentment on their faces, yet they did nothing to stop this travesty of justice.

At the last minute, she turned her head towards Darrow where he stood at the open doorway. "The map!"

she hissed, for she didn't want Nate to overhear. "Don't forget the map!"

They brought her to the lock-up beneath the centuries-old stone court house which sat on the steep hill between Water and Duckworth Streets. As she got out of the car, she was reminded of the time just days ago, when Darrow had stopped her on this very parking lot. Today, though, the car was brought right up to the cellar door beneath the steps linking the two main roads of the old downtown to the tower door which was never warmed by the light of the sun.

This was where they brought the Friday night drunks and brawlers from George Street to cool their heels and sober up, the prostitutes, and the murderers. She wasn't the first woman to be charged for murder to go through this door.

It was the smell inside the tower which was the worst, the smell of centuries of human waste and blood and urine and vomit which had seeped into the cracks of the stone floors and concrete walls. Centuries of every human substance imaginable had been spilled inside this door, but the bleach and lime would never get rid of it. The smell was part of the very stones themselves by now, the smell of despair and lives gone hopelessly wrong.

Despite Laney's rush to arrest her so early in the morning, Carmel was left to cool her heels in the tiny interview room for two hours. It was chilly and bare there, no window to the outside nor color to comfort the eyes. She was glad she'd thrown on a heavy sweater before she left. Her winter coat and her belt had been removed from her possession before being led into the room.

The door opened finally. It was Pam, the legal-aid lawyer, briefcase in hand and professionally attired in black pants and matching blazer. She held a paper tray with two take-out containers of coffee in it.

"Well," she said, sitting opposite Carmel, handing her a cup, "here we are. I was afraid this was going to happen."

"You told me they wouldn't arrest me."

"Yeah," the lawyer said, "I was really hoping they wouldn't."

They stared at each other across the table.

"You didn't do it, though," Pam assured her. "I still believe that."

"Of course I didn't," Carmel exclaimed. "But..."

Pam shook her head. "They still don't have any evidence linking you to the murder," she said, "despite you being at the scene of the crime."

"So why have they arrested me?" After so little sleep last night and the scare, Carmel was feeling quite light-headed and unable to control the panic which had been brewing for two hours during her incarceration in the tiny room. Her voice was rising.

"Calm down," Pam said. "Laney's made the arrest because––well––he's Laney. No one else actually thinks you did it; he's just trying to pin it on you so he can close the case."

"If no one thinks I did it, then I shouldn't be here!"

"And no one disagrees," Pam said in her matter-of-fact voice, remaining calm. "Now, you need to prepare yourself. Laney is about to come in here with all guns blazing, looking for blood. You're not to say a word, no matter how nasty he gets. Let me handle it all."

"But while he has me holed up here, the real killer's on the loose!"

"I realize this is distressing, Carmel," Pam said, leaning over the table and peering at her over her reading glasses. "It's a formality, just remember that."

"I've been arrested," Carmel said. It didn't feel like a formality.

"There is that," Pam replied. "But we'll get you out by the end of the day."

Carmel could only sit back in the orange plastic chair and trust in her counsel.

***

Darrow was left with the map, and he wasn't quite sure what Carmel had wanted him to do with it. She'd mentioned the name Nate O'Reilly, a name familiar to most everyone in the city these days who kept up with the news and the radio call-in shows. The leader of the so-called liberation movement.

Nate O'Reilly was, as far as Darrow could figure, the Newfoundlander's Newfoundlander. A highly educated man, he'd returned to the province with a chip on his shoulder against the establishment because he couldn't break into their ranks. O'Reilly was behind the resurgence of the independence movement, a rabble-rouser. He was a loose cannon, supposedly, but Darrow had never met the man.

And Carmel wanted to enlist this man's help? Darrow shook his head. There had to be a better way.

He examined the map again. It was old, certainly, possibly centuries old. It clearly delineated a small section of coastline somewhere, with what looked like a salt-water pond cut off from the ocean by a beach with a rock formation on it. There were many such formations around the province. He read the words on the map. They meant nothing to him.

What was the point of it and why did Carmel think someone would murder over it? The map itself held no information.

The front door burst open and he was confronted by two men, one of them very angry.

"What have you done with her?" Phonse demanded. His graying curls were covered by a black watch cap against the morning cold, yet he wore only a gray hoodie over his jeans.

The other man leaned on the doorjamb, a solid presence with long hair flowing over his plaid-jacketed shoulders. He folded his arms with satisfaction. "The media is going to hear about this," he said, a slow smile spreading on his face.

"I warned her about getting mixed up with you," Phonse shouted at Darrow. "How can you treat her this way? There's words for men like you!"

"This was a sting of the worst kind," observed the second man, his eyes narrowing as he egged his friend on. Phonse looked ready to take a swing.

Darrow attempted to present a calm manner despite the fact that he himself was still upset about Laney's actions that morning. This could come to blows if he wasn't careful, and the odds of two hefty sober louts against him alone were not in his favor.

He looked Phonse straight in the eye and recognized the common ground between himself and this angry mass of testosterone. They both cared for Carmel, deeply. But the difference between them also shone out, for Phonse could only communicate the depth of his feeling at this moment by thoroughly trouncing Darrow. He saw love, jealousy and helplessness in the other man's eye.

"I share your concern," he said in a quiet and firm voice. "I need your help. *She* needs your help."

When neither man showed signs of budging, the Scotsman's training asserted itself and his authority was unmistakable. "Sit down, for Christ's sake, man! And let's talk about this in a civilized manner."

Darrow waited till they sat. He looked at the second man. "Who are you?" he barked out.

"Nate O'Reilly," the man said as he leaned back and crossed his arms. He spoke with a laid-back assurance which convinced Darrow that he was a force to be reckoned with.

The inspector stared at O'Reilly, recognizing both the name and the figure. This was the man he'd seen in conference with Ruscan Milanovic the morning this had all started, the day of Marcia Flynn's murder.

The very person Carmel had mentioned just moments before she'd been taken away by Laney. Darrow failed to see how this man could help her. In fact, every hackle in his neck was rising, but he'd already let her down too much. Darrow swallowed. He would have to trust her, and so, in turn, trust this O'Reilly fellow.

He would worry about his own case, the bomb threats and Nate O'Reilly's involvement, later. She came first at the moment.

The map was still in his hand. He placed it on the kitchen table when they were all seated. "Have a look at that while I pour the coffee. Tell me what you think." He didn't want to do this, but felt he had no choice. Carmel had specifically brought up Nate's name. Perhaps the younger man had knowledge that could help.

"It's a map?" Phonse's statement came out as a question.

"Yes," Darrow replied. "Carmel found this here in her house."

Nate was silent as he took the paper and studied it closely.

"Hey, Nate, this might be Cap'n Jem's treasure map!" Phonse said, crowding round Nate to look. "You know, the one that was found on the Clerkwell premises? Let me have a look. I can't believe she had it all along and wouldn't give it to me? That little brat! I was going to surprise you with it."

Nate drummed his fingers on the table. "This is only half a map," he said in his deep voice. "This isn't the one found under Water Street, is it?" He looked up at Darrow.

The inspector didn't ask him how he knew this, but nodded and drew their attention to the side of the paper which had been ripped away. "Part of it is missing." He watched them carefully for their reactions.

"It's the other half," Nate said, studying the map again. "The rest of Captain Jem's map."

Phonse screwed up his face, staring at the paper before them. "But I don't understand..."

"Think about it, Phonse," Nate said in his gravelly voice. "Remember Carmel told you the first one they found was only half a map?" He pointed to the X. The other man nodded as a light dawned in his eyes, then his expression clouded over. Their eyes met and Nate silently gave a small shake of his head.

"What are your thoughts?" Darrow asked. The two men knew something.

Nate shifted his attention away from the map and shrugged without making eye contact, wiping his nose with the back of his hand.

"Well, this isn't going to help Carmel get out of jail," Phonse said, leaning back in his wooden chair, sullen again. "It's got nothing to do with that."

"But it's the only thing I have. I thought you two might be able to help clarify things," Darrow said, pressing the point. "Carmel is certain the map is behind the murder."

Nate shrugged as he stood up and looked at his watch. "Nothing to do with us. We'd better get going," he said to Phonse.

With a heavy heart, Inspector Darrow watched from the front door of Carmel's house as the two men hurried down the lane and into Phonse's filthy white truck. He had a feeling he'd just messed up again in a big way, that he should have listened to his instinct and not shared the map with Nate despite what Carmel had asked.

And Nate was certainly the person deep in conversation with Ruscan the morning of Dr. Flynn's death. Ignatius O'Reilly was now a 'person of interest' to Darrow. Unofficially, of course.

Chapter 23

After a gruelling two hours during which Carmel had said very little except to answer the same questions over again, she found herself exhausted now in a grimy little holding cell. A single grated window to the outside was far above her head. The little she could see through it showed only crumbling concrete held together by bright green mold and lichen, with another iron grate above between the sidewalk and the stone of the building. The noise of traffic on Duckworth Street sounded far above her head. She could only picture the lawyers in their black pinstriped court clothes entering the courthouse and the secretaries clip-clopping along to their lunches.

Sitting on the wooden slatted bench which served as bed and chair in the tiny cell, she could only hope that Darrow had taken her meaning and withheld the map from Nate. Did she spell it out for him? She couldn't remember.

The first half of the map found in the old cellar had been of St. Jude Without, Darrow had told her before Marcia's murder. And even though the second half she'd found did not make any sense, for it looked like no landscape she was familiar with, Carmel knew that if Nate was the thief, then when he saw her half of the map he would somehow be able to put the two together. He was from St. Jude Without; he was a Ryan by heritage, and he would also be intimately acquainted with the history of the area. What piece of the puzzle was she missing?

And was she certain that the murderer was also the thief who broke into her house?

"Try to reconstruct the scenario of the murder," she told herself, and closed her eyes to aide her efforts.

She was down in the basement archive. Marcia was busily flipping through the shelves, taking down file folders, placing them on the table. The original map was lying in its Mylar cover, the file folder which enclosed it open. Marcia had grabbed it to her bosom, not letting her inspect it further.

It was no good––she'd been over and over it a thousand times. Marcia speaking, someone answered, she screamed and the lights went out. This wasn't bringing her any closer.

Nate though––Nate. He would have known the legends of Captain Jeremy, having grown up in St. Jude Without. He'd been there when they spoke of the map being found in the hidden cellar under Water Street.

He boasted of knowing how to break into the Rooms, and undoubtedly knew how to bypass the locked system in order to get access to the archives.

But how would he have known Marcia was down there? Had he simply waited in the broom closet or the electrical room until she passed by?

She lay down on the hard wooden bench and tried to sleep, but there was no solace for her that day.

***

Darrow hadn't been at his desk long before he was informed that the bomb-threat case might have been taken up a significant notch. There was a report of an explosion over in a lane off Cabot Street, loss of life as yet undetermined.

Arriving on the scene just yards away from the RNC headquarters, Darrow pushed his way past the throng of neighbors and other on-lookers, then past the fire-trucks and ambulances, all with their lights ablaze. The constable on duty lifted up the police tape for him to pass under.

He stopped and looked all around him, at the cluster of old houses which were struggling to become gentrified but just couldn't seem to haul themselves up the property ladder. In the present economic climate, these tiny houses couldn't command the high prices their renovators dreamt of, as no amount of granite countertops and rooftop decks could ever cancel out the squalor of the neighboring crack houses and squats. The down-and-outs had to live somewhere, and they preferred the city center.

The structure used to be a wooden stables built back before automobiles had become common on the streets, probably before the First World War. It had morphed into a garage in the intervening years. Little paint remained on the sagging clapboard of the side which was on the verge of collapsing, for the roof which had held it together was just about gone. It had once had a window in the large door but the glass now lay in shards around them. The garage had been attached on one side, with less than a yard of clearance between it and the house next door on the other side.

The blast had taken little toll on the two neighboring houses. Fortunately, they appeared to have contained the brunt of the explosive. Directly behind the garage, had only been a rock cliff which had also helped stop the force of the blast spreading to the heavily populated area behind and up the steep hill. Directly in front of the garage was an empty lot, opening the cul de sac to the same view of the South Side Hills as from Darrow's own office. Situated on the side of the steep hill overlooking the harbor as it was and due to its central location, this little enclave might have been sought after property in any other city.

The fire caused by the explosion had been quickly put out by the prompt action of the fire department. Loose papers, half-burnt and soggy, floated in the gusts of the March wind.

Darrow knew the officer in charge, and quickly explained why he was called to the location.

"What's the damage, Mackey?" Darrow tersely asked the officer in charge.

"This is it," the man said, spreading his arms. "There doesn't appear to be any loss of life. No one was in the garage at the time of the explosion." He pointed to a spot where the garage had sat, now a mass of wreckage. Two firemen and a police woman were scrabbling amongst the debris. "They're finding evidence of a makeshift laboratory."

"A meth lab?"

Mackey shook his head. "Not by the looks of it."

Darrow reached down and picked up a large scrap of paper lying wet on the ground, taking it gingerly between his gloved fingers. It was familiar, for he'd seen this same image plastered around town in the last week, the posters with the letters NLA in dripping red on a black background.

"How about the neighbors--what do they know of this?" Darrow looked towards the house on his right. Three women of various ages and states of undress were gathered on the tiny steps leading to the front door, last night's makeup still evident on their faces as they talked excitedly to anyone within reach.

"Those three rent rooms in that house," Mackey told him. "They call themselves night-shift workers, however, they've all spent time in the lock-up before, if you know what I mean."

"Ah," said Darrow. "Ladies of the night-shift."

Mackey nodded. "Although the garage was attached to their house, they claim not to know anything about it, said they weren't aware of anyone using the garage," he said. "And I believe them."

"And next-door?" That structure didn't look too promising. All the windows and doors were securely boarded up and judging by the weathered look of the plywood, had been so for some time.

Mackey consulted his notes. "The old couple who lived there passed away ten-odd years ago, no wills," he said. "The house has been empty and in limbo ever since, with all ten of the children arguing about who gets what."

"With ten of them to split it up between, I doubt if there'd be much left over after paying the lawyers," Darrow said, shaking his head.

"Ain't that the truth," Mackey said. "Oh, there's another person on the street, a sweet old woman down the road. One of those who don't have anything to do but look out the window all day. You might want to talk with her."

He found the lady in question and, shocked as she was, she was able to provide insight as to the recent comings and goings in the small lane. There was a huge explosion, she said, and then a purple cloud. She looked at Darrow as if she was afraid he'd laugh at her, consider her senile, but he nodded encouragingly. Men had been at the garage, she then told Darrow, off and on for the past week. The padlock had been cut off, didn't look like they had a key. No, she'd had no idea what they were up to. A single elderly woman on her own didn't like to ask questions.

Darrow approached the firemen who were examining the wreckage of the garage.

"Definite traces of iodine," he was told.

That confirmed they were dealing with ammonium nitrogen triiodide––an extremely volatile substance. It was the mark of a sophisticated bomber who had half a clue what he was doing. Disgruntled students might make the old Molotov Cocktail, while terrorists favored simple ammonium nitrate. But this substance required patience and careful watching to make sure it stayed damp. Once the triiodide compound dried out too much, the slightest breath could set it off, a feather touch, even the heat from the weak March sun through a garage window. The purple flume of smoke witnessed by the old lady was further proof of the substance.

More than ever, he needed to get Ruscan Milanovic in for questioning.

***

There was little work being done at the desk of Inspector John Darrow that afternoon. Once he'd overseen operations at the bomb-site and ascertained that it was connected to the recent bomb scares and the NLA, officers were dispatched to bring Ruscan in for questioning.

As he waited, he attempted to write up his report but couldn't concentrate on it, his mind was on Carmel. He knew that Laney didn't have any strong evidence to charge her for Evelyn had kept him well informed, yet he still felt he had failed the woman he held in high esteem, a woman whose company he enjoyed and wanted more of, her of the quirky smile and bold curiosity... Because of him she was jailed on murder charges.

Evelyn Wright entered his office uninvited and sat on the padded visitor's chair across from him. She placed a coffee before him.

"It's my fault," he stated.

She shook her head, but without much conviction. "It's Laney; you know how he gets a bee in his bonnet and can't see beyond his nose."

"No," he said. "I allowed this to happen. If I'd handled Laney better right from the beginning and didn't allow this resentment to grow. If I'd been more circumspect with Carmel, if Laney didn't know I was seeing her, he wouldn't have overstepped himself and arrested her. He would have waited until he had the evidence in hand."

"John for God's sake, you're entitled to a life," Evelyn replied, not holding back. "And none of us can help letting Laney under our skins––he's that sort of idiot. Don't blame yourself for that."

"She's sitting in a jail cell, wrongfully accused."

"So what are you going to do about it?"

"I tried to enlist Nate O'Reilly's help, as she asked," Darrow told her. "Against my better judgement. But he was no use. And I don't see what her map has to do with it all."

"Seriously––the guy from the Newfoundland Liberation Army? Nate O'Reilly's involved in this?" Evelyn laughed. "He'd make a better murder suspect than

Carmel. Is there any way we can wrap him up and give him to Laney?"

Darrow stared at her as the realization struck. "Oh dear God," he said, "did I misinterpret her? Maybe she was saying she suspected Nate. I've really made a balls-up of this."

"Oh come on," Evelyn said with a sharpness in her voice. "It's not all about you. Anyway, she should be out of there by now. Laney has no evidence built up yet. The Public Prosecutor won't let him keep her."

"I do appreciate you staying on the case," he said. "It's not easy working with Laney."

"I hate being part of his team," Evelyn said. "He makes us all look bad."

After a pause, she continued, "So? Shouldn't you be somewhere else right now?"

He looked at his watch, then back to Sergeant Wright with a blank question in his eyes.

"Carmel's getting out of the lock-up," she pointed out. "She may need some support?"

"Do you really think that's advisable?" he asked. "Hender's already had a go at me about all this. I've done enough damage to Carmel already with Laney thinking he can get at me through her."

"I can't believe you're saying that," she said with a touch of exasperation. "Do you hear yourself? I already said, it's not all about you. I can't put it much plainer than that."

He stared at her as he realized finally what she was saying and might have blushed with embarrassment if he was able.

"I've been a selfish pig, haven't I?" he asked. "Worrying about how her situation reflects on me professionally. She needs me."

"Praise God, he sees the light!"

He loosened his tie. "I can't be uninvolved in this case and it was wrong of me to think I had to pretend to be." Standing up, he grabbed his coat from the rack and shrugged it on. "If anyone's looking for me, I won't be back this afternoon."

He ran in an almost straight line down the stairs from Harvey Road to Long's Hill, then down further to the courthouse and on down more stairs to the Water Street entrance of the lock-up. Darrow was slow off the mark today, however, and someone had already beaten him to it.

David Clerkwell stood with Pam, Carmel's Legal-Aid lawyer in the foyer.

"I was going to post bail for her," David said when he saw Darrow, his eyes flittering in the police officer's direction. "But Pam got her out."

"It wasn't me so much," replied Pam. "They have no case against her yet, nothing to hang it on. I told her it would just be a matter of time. They've had to stay the charges."

Darrow looked at the two. Pam he knew and respected from her work within the justice system, but David Clerkwell was another matter, having only met the man recently. He knew the young man had family money and had made a name for himself early around town and the archival circles. Yet Darrow had found David cold, and didn't trust the way the man never made eye contact. This caring side seemed out of character.

Or maybe, he realized, just maybe he was jealous that a mere work colleague of Carmel's was showing more compassion, more caring than he had himself. Darrow was having a very uncomfortable day.

"I knew they couldn't drag this out too long," Darrow agreed. His back was turned to the lock-up door, and he didn't see Carmel being led out as he spoke.

But David did, and was quick to be by her side. Darrow didn't like how David embraced the woman as she walked out of the door to the lock-up. It was a quick light touch around her, certainly not the embrace of a lover, but still.

"I hated the thought of you locked up in there; I know how it affects you," David said softly. "I felt so bad." His arms had barely touched her before releasing her.

She looked a mess. Hair wild and dark shadows under her eyes, she glared at Darrow. "What do you mean you knew this wasn't going to stick?" she asked. "Why didn't you do something about it earlier?" Pam slipped quietly away. David remained, but held himself back, carefully watching the unjoyful reunion between Darrow and Carmel while pretending he wasn't.

"You let me get hauled into jail, then questioned for hours," Carmel continued. "You knew the charges wouldn't stick, but you let Laney do this?" She couldn't believe it. This man who said he cared for her had let her rot in a jail cell for the majority of the day. She was so exhausted she wasn't even thinking straight.

Darrow pulled her aside. "We had no choice in the matter," he said to her in a low voice. His hair was standing on end––it hadn't been brushed when he received the text from Constable Brown, and it was the last thing on his mind now.

But Carmel wasn't finding his dishevelment charming at this moment. She didn't know what he'd been going through, only that she had been left alone with no one save Pam, a paid lawyer, on her side.

"And another thing I need to tell you," he said. His Scots accent was strong as he looked at her with concern. "I showed Nate O'Reilly the map."

Her jaw opened. This was too much. "You did what?"

"I thought you wanted me to tell him!"

"How could you betray me like that?"

"You weren't very precise in your instructions," he fired back. "I couldn't read your mind."

"Well, did you arrest him?"

"For what?"

"The murder!"

"There's no evidence for that!"

"But it had to be him," she said, and turned away.

Chapter 24

As David drove her along Winsor Lake, a flurry of snow whipped round his SUV.

"I appreciate you doing this," she said. Exhausted even more now, she could hardly think. Darrow had disappointed her. The break-in and lack of sleep last night and the arrest this morning had done her in. And she realized she was starving. But all she wanted was to lie on her bed with all the doors locked tight and disappear into her pillows.

"It's the least I can do," David murmured, carefully watching the twists in the road along the water's edge. "I'm just so sorry about the whole thing."

"It's not your fault," she replied, thinking of Darrow as she said it. It wasn't Darrow's fault either, really, but did he have to be so dense? So high and mighty, so professional. Couldn't he stop being a cop for a while and undo that tie?

"No," said David, "it probably is. I just hate to see you involved."

She lay her head back against the headrest. The warmth from the heated seat was spreading and making her drowsy so she could hardly keep her eyes open. "I can't believe Darrow showed him the map," she said.

"What map is that?"

"The one from the red book," she mumbled. She was going to tell him more, but that was the last thing she remembered until David gently shook her awake and helped her up the steps to her home. She found he had stopped for brownies at the bakery along the way, for he knew they were her favourites.

He put the kettle on as soon as they were inside the house, then turned to look outside the kitchen window. The snow had melted from the branches and off behind them, old gravestones cast their shadows in the sun.

"There are fairies back there," he said and he turned back to Carmel.

"Rumors of," she said, pulling her heavy sweater over her head. She wanted to do nothing more than lie down and wished he would leave again. She didn't want to talk about fairies or treasure chests or maps or ghosts or murders, she just wanted it all to go away.

"I suppose the ground is quite frozen still," he continued. "I don't suppose we could go out and have a look?"

She mustered the energy to lift her head. First the basement, then the attic, now the graveyard? David was possibly the nosiest person she'd ever met. Aside from herself. "Now? What do you want to go out there for? It's cold out, and there's still snow on the ground."

He shrugged and gave a small deprecating laugh. "Sorry. Let's get the tea made and get you looked after instead, okay?"

She watched him pour the boiling water into the pot. "Tina," she said.

His back stiffened, but he turned to face her with a smile. "Tina. What about her?"

"What's on the go between you two? She makes you feel uncomfortable, yet you allow her... I mean, you didn't stop her from coming to dinner that night, even though neither of us wanted her there. You could have said no."

David looked at her with those remarkable eyes, so similar to yet at the same time so different from Tina's. "She claims to be my half-sister," he told her. "She wants so much to be a Clerkwell."

"I don't understand," Carmel said. "Was she black-mailing you or something?"

"In a way," he replied, bringing the teapot to the table. "Of course, I know it's nonsense, and she has no way to prove it. But still... It's just easier to not make waves."

As she slumped at the kitchen table, unsure whether she had the strength to go upstairs to bed, David stood across from her, fingering the old map.

"This is the map from the red book you were speaking about?" he asked in his soft voice.

Had she mentioned it? Yes, of course she had, when she was half asleep on the ride home. "Yeah, it came out of the book, the one that was stolen last night." A yawn overtook her.

"I don't understand this." He was studying it closely.

"No, it doesn't make sense, does it? Two old half maps, and they don't go together. What are the odds of that?"

He gave a sigh of frustration. "You must know something more about this," he said. "Haven't you researched it?"

"David, I just found it early this morning," she said as her patience finally hit the boiling point. "After I woke up with an intruder standing over me. Then I was hauled off to jail and have been there most of the day. It's the lock-up, not an internet cafe!"

He switched the charm on again, but it was a half-hearted attempt. "Sorry, I'm being single-minded again," he said. "Maybe I'll just leave you to recuperate."

She quickly closed the front door behind him, not seeing that he was already bent over his phone.

Back in her cold house with the hot tea in front of her after her outburst, she felt curiously revived. Carmel stared at the half of a map in her hands. It wasn't telling her anything except there was a mysterious treasure buried somewhere under a rock formation.

The missing half must hold the clue. But it had disappeared from the archives after Marcia's untimely death. She again tried to imagine the two pieces together. She'd been assured that the first was probably of St. Jude Without, but the second piece didn't fit.

She stared at it till her eyes hurt, and she traced the line of the coast. Yes, there was the shore in a similar shape to Snellen's Field, but there all similarity ended to the view she could see out her window.

Instead of dipping into the tiny cove between the field and the point where the ponies grazed amid the cottages, the beach continued in a straight line with what looked like a pond where that cove was now. Squinting, she could see some words written by the pond in an old copperplate script.

"Faery Pond? You have to be kidding me." She sat back in disgust. This was not a real map, it was someone's imagination at work here. It bore no resemblance to the real landscape of St. Jude Without. The fairies lived up in the graveyard behind her house. Supposedly.

Although marked on the (imaginary) beach there was a rock formation, it looked to be in the shape of a large dog. And below that dog was an X. It didn't reflect the reality of the community's coast line. None of it made sense.

Carmel needed to talk with someone who knew the history of St. Jude Without. Someone who'd been around for a while. Someone who knew everything about everyone, who probably knew the origins of every roadside boulder. Someone who might, if they were buttered up enough, explain the meaning of this half map.

Vee Ryan. She almost threw up in her mind at the thought of asking her for help.

Maybe Phonse instead? No. Or Bridget? She hadn't seen much of her friend lately, possibly Ian had returned. Best not bother her.

Vee. It had to be Phonse's harridan of a mother.

But she couldn't go empty-handed––she would need something with which to sweeten up the old bat in order to be allowed in through the door. David's brownies would have to be sacrificed.

***

The wind had picked up from the north as it hitched a ride down the Labrador Current from Greenland, and it cut through the seams of her coat like a razor. On this exposed bit of ground, the snow could never stick around long and only ice remained in the ruts and along the broken grasses on the sides of the road. Carmel paused at the head of the lane leading down the point and to the house where Phonse lived with his mother. His truck was gone, so it would be the two of them alone. She almost turned back at the thought.

But she forced herself to trudge along the stones, brownies held high like a white flag for the enemy to hold their fire. At the back door to the cottage, she hesitated, almost knocked. But she knew she'd never make it past the artillery in that manner, so she took a deep breath and walked on in the door as if expecting a welcome.

A small TV blared the theme to *Another World*. Was that soap still running after all these years? The kitchen remained as she had seen it last summer on the news during Vee's fifteen minutes of fame with a local reporter. Done in the style of dated kitsch, it hadn't seen changes since Phonse was in diapers. Hand-carved gingerbread surrounded the window with its lace curtain drawn tight against passing ships, and various china kittens and angels decorated the tiny shelves. There was a pervading odor of bleach in the room.

Vee herself was ensconced at the formica table, cup of tea in hand and hair in the usual rollers. The look on her face at seeing Carmel on her doorstep was almost worth the price of admission.

"He's not here!" Vee screeched right away. She thought for a moment. "How come you're not in jail?"

"Because I didn't do it. And I don't want Phonse," Carmel replied. "It's you I need to talk to."

"I'm busy," Vee said. "I'm watching my story."

"Surely to God that's a re-run," Carmel said. "Hasn't that show been off the air for twenty years or so?"

"Phonse got me the DVDs of the whole series for Christmas. I can watch it whenever I want to." Vee stuck her chin in the air as she paused the show. "What do you want?"

"I brought brownies."

"They're store-bought," Vee said with a sniff after examining the package.

Carmel opened the plastic wrap to let the smell of the freshly baked goods waft out.

"I allows they're probably better than what you'd make, anyway." Dislike for Carmel and greed were battling in her beady eyes. The brownies were winning, as Carmel suspected they would.

"How was Florida?" Carmel asked as she sat, uninvited. Vee had spent the winter down south, her first ever Christmas away from her son Phonse. It had been a difficult time for him.

"Hot. Nothing to do there," she grumbled. "Won't be going there again. Spent my whole time worrying about the lad, especially when I heard you got mixed up in more murders." She took the largest brownie out of the package and set to it.

Vee was still the same pasty white she'd been before she left for the south. "You didn't get out in the sun much, then?"

"Indeed not," she said around the chocolaty goodness. "And that's how I keep my complexion. You wouldn't have all those horrible freckles if you stayed out of the sun."

Take a deep breath, Carmel told herself. *Your freckles are cute and attractive. She is neither of those things. Never was, never will be.*

"So, I need your help," she told the older woman, judging that enough time had passed for the sugar to work its way into Vee's bloodstream. She took the map and placed it on the table. "What can you tell me about this?"

'What's that then?"

"That's what I'm asking you," Carmel said, fixing a smile on her face. "Does this look familiar at all?"

Vee took the paper in her chocolate-smeared fingers. "What's that say? The Faerie Pond?"

Carmel nodded.

"Hmph." But Vee continued to stare at the map. "That's what it looked like, back then. I remember it."

"You know this place?" Carmel asked, hardly believing what she'd heard.

"Should do," Vee said. "It's just up there around the corner isn't it? Only we call it Fairy Pond Beach now, cause there's no pond anymore."

"Fairy Pond Beach," Carmel repeated. "You do mean the little cove between Snellen's Field and the point, right? I never knew it had a name."

"You wouldn't know because you're not from here," Vee said, as if that were Carmel's main problem to begin with. "Used to be a little pond there, and the Iron Dog, yes, they have the dog there too. My father used to have photos of it––don't know where they got to."

"What happened to the pond and the rock formation, then?" Carmel asked her. "Must have been a pretty bad storm to wash those away."

"Wasn't no storm!" Vee had finished her second brownie by now and sated, could afford to let her scorn rise again. "My dear, that was the British, now, wasn't it?"

"You're going to have to explain," Carmel said. "I'm not from here, remember?"

"Well, you know the iron mines on Bell Island?"

Carmel nodded. The island across from them had once been a thriving iron ore mine with operations running deep below the ocean floor. It had at one time been the jewel in Newfoundland's crown. The ore in the mine had since dried up, or at least there were cheaper places to extract it now.

"During the second world war, the Germans were bombing the ships that came to take the ore," Vee said. "Mind, I was just a child at the time."

"St. John's harbor had a net strung across it to keep the German U-boats out," Carmel said, retrieving a long lost tidbit from her memory.

"Well, we saw more action here," Vee said boastfully. "I recall the night it happened, I was just five years old. First in September the Lord Stracona and the Saganaga were attacked and sunk, right out there in the tickle. Twenty-nine men died there, that morning. And then later in November one night, the Germans blew up a couple more ships loading at the dock. Twas a terrible thing to see in the pitch black, just over there in the water."

Vee stared out the kitchen window at the ocean and Bell Island beyond. Carmel could now understand why she kept the lace curtains between the cozy kitchen and the memories of the devastations on the ocean all those years ago. "The burning boats lit the night, and the screams of the drowning men carried over the water. You could see every detail of the cliffs so clearly from the fires."

It was one thing to read about the devastation caused by the wars, but they had been in Europe, a half a world and a lifetime removed from herself here and now. Listening to Vee's first-hand account was like the first time she'd seen color photos of the concentration camp liberations––as if the changeover from monotone to color removed the wall of time between then and now.

"I had no idea," Carmel said, her voice soft and slow.

"We were British then," Vee said, meaning the time before confederation with Canada. "And the British tried to get the U-Boat that had done all that. But he slipped away underwater and they misfired, and ended up getting the Iron Dog instead."

"That must have been right outside your bedroom window," Carmel said, realizing the layout of the tiny bungalow. "Just over the field from where you lay."

The older woman nodded and reached for another brownie. "It was a terrible frightful night. We didn't have much heart for the bonfires of Guy Fawkes Night, a couple of days after, I can tell you. That was the only year ever there wasn't a good torching on Bonfire Night in St. Jude Without."

"So the Iron Dog and the fairy pond were destroyed that night."

"Indeed," Vee said. "I barely remembers them myself."

Carmel contemplated the map, her finger on the narrow strip of land between the pond and the ocean, where the dog was marked.

"I thought," Carmel hesitated. "I thought the fairies lived up by the graveyard, behind my house. And wasn't I told that fairies don't like the ocean?" Not that she believed in the fairies. Of course not. But according to legend... And there were those mysterious twinkling lights last fall.

Vee stared at her over her glasses as if she'd all of a sudden grown ten heads. "I guess they was salt-water fairies, then," she said, daring her to mock. "And of course they had to move up the hill, their home had been blown up."

"Ah," Carmel said. "Of course. And the iron... I thought fairies hated iron, too." Her hand strayed toward the packet of brownies which were quickly shuffled out of her reach and tidied away into the old bread box on the counter.

"Was that all you wanted? You'd best be gone then, I got things to do." Vee ignored her last challenge and turned back to her TV. "Now where's my clicker-box?"

Carmel handed her the TV remote and took her leave.

Chapter 25

D arrow had retraced his steps up Long's Hill again almost as fast as his earlier descent, and his mind was working as furiously as his lungs. Nate O'Reilly as the murderer?

Yes, the man had been hanging out near The Rooms on the morning of Dr. Flynn's murder, and in the company of Ruscan Milanovic. Those two together could never be up to any good. He pictured them again at the Tim Horton's, their heads bent close.

And Nate was a descendant of Captain Jem, and part of the St. Jude Without family. If the murder was about the maps as Carmel insisted, then it was logical that Nate would feel he had a claim to any treasure buried by that pirate. And Nate had big political plans which would require massive funding if he was going to pit himself against the big guys already in power.

Nate knew the layout of the archives, knew all the ins and outs of the building, and had reason to hold a grudge against Dr. Flynn.

Darrow reached the top of the steps onto Harvey Road and paused to catch his breath. Before him lay the coffee shop with the RNC Headquarters behind it, and looming over all, The Rooms. From here, he could see the iron gate that led to the basement fire door which had been alarming after Marcia's death, an easy enough barrier to scale for one in a hurry. Despite the heavily trafficked road, there had been no witnesses to the escape.

But he couldn't stop long. The murder of Marcia Flynn was not his circus, the players were not his monkeys. He had amends to make with Carmel.

His car was parked as always in his slot outside the RNC building, and he chose the fastest, most direct route out of town towards Portugal Cove. The traffic lights were with him all the way as he headed west into the sun.

As North Point Road turned to gravel just before Snellen's Field, he glanced down towards the water and slowed the car, for his eye was caught by the layout of the small beach between the field and the point of land stretching beyond. In that tiny cove––an inlet really––the water was protected from the wind, and the waves did not reach it, though the whitecaps rose threateningly just beyond in the more open water of the tickle from the hurricane force winds the night before. He pictured again the map Carmel had found in her house, and it matched with what he saw before him. The Fairy Pond had been located at the bottom of Snellen's Field, once upon a time when Captain Jem was a living, breathing man.

It was then he realized he was not alone on this gravelled road. A vehicle was parked facing him on the wrong side of the road, hauled off as if the driver had been in a hurry to stop. He walked over to the vehicle. It was empty, save for a red book half-lying under a blanket in the back seat, the leather cover worn on the edges. Darrow didn't need to look at the title to recognize it.

And down there in Snellen's Field, before it dipped to a small cliff and the ocean below, stood a burly man in a checked jacket, his long hair whipped by the wind.

Nate O'Reilly turned to watch Darrow's descent.

"Cabot Street," Darrow said when he caught up.

Nate nodded. "I heard," he said. "Could be any of a number of the idiots. I told them they were going too far." He gave a sigh.

"Milanovic?"

"He's unhinged," Nate said in his deep rumbly voice as he shook his head. "I didn't want anything to do with him."

"Who murdered Flynn?"

The burly man pointed his chin toward the water. Darrow could make out a figure sitting on the boulders below the field.

***

Once outside, Carmel hesitated then wandered across the point to the place where the Iron Dog had sat for thousands of years, the accidental artistry of a careless glacier, guarding the salt-water pond of the fairies of St. Jude Without. The rock formation had just as carelessly been blown apart by friendly fire all those years ago.

The snow was thin over the frozen grass and the ponies skittered away at her approach. With gray sky overhead, and the ocean water grayer still, she could smell the diesel of the ferry as it chugged its way across the tickle to Bell Island.

Tina. Possibly the illicit offspring of one of the Clerkwell's, which explained her deep interest in the family's history, along with the barbed remarks thrown between the young woman and David. Tina, who resented David's entitlement, who felt entitled herself to something from the family. Could that young slight woman have wielded the strength to heft the iron doorstop and kill Marcia Flynn?

When she reached the end, Carmel stared at where the old beachline was marked on the map. There was little to show for what had been there on the surface, but below the water, the bedrock still showed. The British warship must have hit the boulder formation exactly spot on as if it were a target, tearing up the shore and gouging the beach right out of it. The rocks around glowed rusty against the yellowed grasses, the last remnants of the old dog's bones.

If Captain Jeremy had buried his wife's dowry of jewels and coins under the Iron Dog as the map stated, then the treasure was long gone, scattered by the blast in 1942 and washed out to sea. Maybe the necklaces and tiaras now adorned the mermaids in the depths, the coins now were covered with barnacles and had become part of the underwater eco-system, just like the wrecked ships further out.

She became aware of another person, felt the stare of eyes on her bowed head, and she looked up across the water to the beach which bordered Snellen's Field.

"David," she said, recognizing the gray eyes beneath the drawn hood of the all-weather jacket. Of course, it was David all along. How could it have been anyone else? Only he had access to the archive basement. David, the descendant of that long-ago Clerkwell son whose bride and dowry had been stolen right from under his nose by the ancestor of her friends in St. Jude Without. Family memories lived long in this land.

He looked sorrowfully over the water at her. "It's all gone," he said over the short distance. He climbed down from the rocks and to the edge of the sea itself. There, he scuffed the small pebbles, as if looking underneath them to uncover the lost treasure, looking for a hint of the gold.

"It's all gone, David," she agreed. "It was all for nothing, then, wasn't it?"

He shook his head. "I'm so sorry," he said. "You know I never meant to involve you. You shouldn't have been downstairs, you should have had time to get back upstairs. I'd asked you to hurry. When I heard your voice in the back, I just panicked. I didn't mean to kill her; I was just going to creep up behind her, throw the sack over her head and take the map, make it look like it was an outside job."

"But... why? Why go to all that trouble? It was just a piece of paper. You would have seen it eventually."

David looked up at her. "She wasn't sharing it. And it's my map," he said simply, across the water. "The treasure that Jeremy Ryan stole belonged to my family."

"It belonged to Eliza," Carmel reminded him. "It was her dowry, according to the Ryan family legends."

"Well, the Clerkwell family stories say differently," he replied, a touch of haughtiness in his voice. "She and her dowry were stolen from my family. It was all ours by right, and I couldn't risk anyone else finding it. Marcia was so greedy, she didn't know what she had, but she suspected it was valuable. She gave me no choice."

"And the fire alarm? You set that off to make it look like it was someone from the outside."

"Yes, that was all part of the original plan," he said, brightening a little at the memory.

"It was you who broke into my house that night?"

"You kept the map from me."

Carmel shook her head. "David, I still don't understand," she said.

"You wouldn't," he said, turning nasty again. "You have no family, nothing to be proud of. You're nothing but an assistant."

Behind his head, Carmel saw Darrow and Nate O'Reilly making their way down the slope.

"You only befriended me because of the map," Carmel said. For some reason, this hurt more than being framed for a murder she didn't commit. "I thought... I really thought I was special. It felt like you were my only friend when everyone else was against me."

He lifted his head and stared at her directly in the eye. "Friends?" He spoke as if the word was a foreign concept.

Darrow and Nate reached the small cliff's edge of Snellen's Field above David's head.

"They've come for me, haven't they?" His voice was soft.

Carmel nodded.

He hesitated, darting a glance to his left along the rocky shore as if considering his chances of making a break for it, then he pulled himself upright and turned to meet his consequences.

Chapter 26

"**A**re you sure we can be seen out in public together now?"

"Frankly, I don't care," Darrow said.

They were sitting side by side on a bench in the tiny park overlooking the water, both their gazes set toward the narrow harbor entrance. Signal Hill was alight in the last of the sun's rays from the west, as were the crumbling concrete fortifications of Fort Amherst across the Narrows, just up from where the giant net had been strung in hopes of catching the U-boats all those years ago.

"I know you're not a murderer," he continued. "Even if we can't prove that David is, you're still in the clear." He lifted his arm to place around her shoulder and she nestled in.

A child's unhappy cry sounded to their right. The old rust-colored dog had discovered a family with four small children who were having an impromptu outside picnic on this warmish evening.

"Irn!" Darrow barked out. The Newfoundland looked up from where he was licking up the last of the fallen food, even the garlic sauce, then with a satisfied grin loped back to the two. He sat at Carmel's feet and laid his heavy head on her knee.

Irn with his rusty coat, hot garlicky breath and smile as wide as his face. She was glad to have this living iron dog by her side to banish the dogs of metal and stone which had haunted her life in the past week. Even the patch of drool quickly spreading on her knee was welcome.

"I thought, at one point, I thought it might be Tina who killed Marcia," Carmel said as she ruffled the old dog's fur. "She was really creeping me out, always tagging along with me and David. He would never say anything to her, even though it was obvious he didn't want her along."

"She may be a half-sister or cousin to him," Darrow remarked. "Her mother used to work for his family firm. She lost her job when she became pregnant, and couldn't get another job in the city. The Clerkwell family has a long reach. It was the end of her, and she went downhill quickly."

Carmel nodded. "I guess Tina was jealous of him. He said she was sort of blackmailing him, in a passive-aggressive way."

"He wouldn't have wanted that rumor to spread."

"And Nate," she continued, after a pause. "I really wanted him to be the murderer. Guess I just don't like him, and that got in the way of my thinking."

"Looks like he'll be sticking around the cove for a while yet," Darrow observed. "Of course, with a restless spirit like his, he may not be around for long."

"And speaking of restless spirits..."

Darrow laughed. "Milanovic is gone for good."

"Thank God," she said with a sigh of relief. "It doesn't say much for my taste in men, I'm afraid."

She felt rather than heard the rumble of his laughter as he squeezed her closer. "That remains to be proven."

Carmel looked up at his warm brown eyes. She reached up her hand and drew his face down towards hers. His lips were surprisingly soft. "Yes," she said. "That remains to be proven."

The end

***

The story of Carmel, Darrow and the crowd of *St. Jude Without* continues in **St. Jude Undone**, Book 4 of the series.

Available in Ebook, Paper Back, Large Print and Audiobooks direct from the author at LizGraham.ca or from all major retailers.

Thank you for purchasing this book. If you would like a personally signed
book plate, feel visit LizGraham.ca to order!

MORE BOOKS BY LIZ (E M) GRAHAM:

WITCH KIN CHRONICLES (E M GRAHAM)
·An Ignorant Witch, Book 1
·An Arrogant Witch, Book 2
·An Errant Witch, Book 3
·An Obstinate Witch, Book 4
·An Enigmatic Witch, Book 5
·An Embittered Witch, Book 6

CARMEL MCALISTAIR MYSTERIES (LIZ GRAHAM)
·The Cut Throat
·The Garrote
·The Iron Dog
·St. Jude Undone

OTHERS (LIZ GRAHAM)
·An Imperfect Death (The Unlikely Heroine)
·The Auction (An Unlikely Short Story)
·A Northern Romance
·Man from La Manche

All books are available in Ebook, PaperBack, Large Print and Audio formats
from LizGraham.ca or through your favorite retailer.

www.ingramcontent.com/pod-product-compliance
Lightning Source LLC
Chambersburg PA
CBHW030816020726
47499CB00006B/1946